A Nest for Celeste

HENRY COLE

A Nest for Celeste

A Story About Art, Inspiration, and the Meaning of Home

KATHERINE TEGEN BOOKS
An Imprint of HarperCollins Publishers

Katherine Tegen Books is an imprint of HarperCollins Publishers.

A Nest for Celeste: A Story About Art, Inspiration, and the Meaning of Home

Copyright © 2010 by Henry Cole

For information address HarperCollins Children's Books, a division of HarperCollins Publishers,

10 East 53rd Street, New York, NY 10022.

www.harpercollinschildrens.com

Library of Congress Cataloging-in-Publication Data

Cole, Henry, date

A nest for Celeste / Henry Cole. — 1st ed.

p.   cm.

Summary: Celeste, a mouse longing for a real home, becomes a source of inspiration to teenaged

Joseph, assistant to the artist and naturalist John James Audubon, at a New Orleans, Louisiana,

plantation in 1821.

ISBN 978-0-06-170410-9 (trade bdg. : alk. paper)

ISBN 978-0-06-170411-6 (lib. bdg.: alk. paper)

[1. Mice—Fiction. 2. Mason, Joseph, 1807-1883—Childhood and youth—Fiction.

3. Human-animal relationships—Fiction. 4. Artists—Fiction. 5. Home—Fiction.

6. Audubon, John James, 1785-1851—Fiction. 7. New Orleans (La.)—History—

19th century—Fiction.] I. Title.

PZ7.C67728Nes 2010   2009011813

[Fic]—dc22   CIP

                                                                                        AC

Typography by Amy Ryan

10 11 12 13 14   CG/RRDB   10 9 8 7 6 5 4 3 2 1

❖ First Edition

CONTENTS

One	*The Basket Maker*	11
Two	*Illianna and Trixie*	17
Three	*Mr. Audubon*	21
Four	*A Sudden Departure*	30
Five	*A Narrow Escape*	49
Six	*A New Nest*	57
Seven	*Rescue by Dash*	67
Eight	*Joseph*	77
Nine	*A Friend*	83
Ten	*Feet in the Gravy*	92
Eleven	*A Portrait*	104
Twelve	*Pigeons*	111
Thirteen	*The River*	120
Fourteen	*A Close One*	129
Fifteen	*The Ivory-Billed*	140

Sixteen	*Cornelius*	149
Seventeen	*Outside*	167
Eighteen	*The Storm*	177
Nineteen	*Aftermath*	185
Twenty	*Lafayette*	189
Twenty-one	*The Gondola*	199
Twenty-two	*Lafayette Returns*	203
Twenty-three	*Flight*	209
Twenty-four	*A Homecoming,* *and Inspiration*	221
Twenty-five	*Cornelius Says Adieu*	231
Twenty-six	*The Attic*	241
Twenty-seven	*A Friend Returns*	249
Twenty-eight	*Lafayette Strikes a Pose*	264
Twenty-nine	*Freedom*	275

THIRTY	A Discovery	279
THIRTY-ONE	Housecleaning	285
THIRTY-TWO	A Homecoming of Sorts	293
THIRTY-THREE	An Unwanted Housemate	300
THIRTY-FOUR	Trixie Takes Off . . .	307
THIRTY-FIVE	. . . Like a Rock Tossed Into a Muddy Pond	310
THIRTY-SIX	Back from New Orleans	319
THIRTY-SEVEN	Departure	325
AFTERWORD		339

A Nest for Celeste

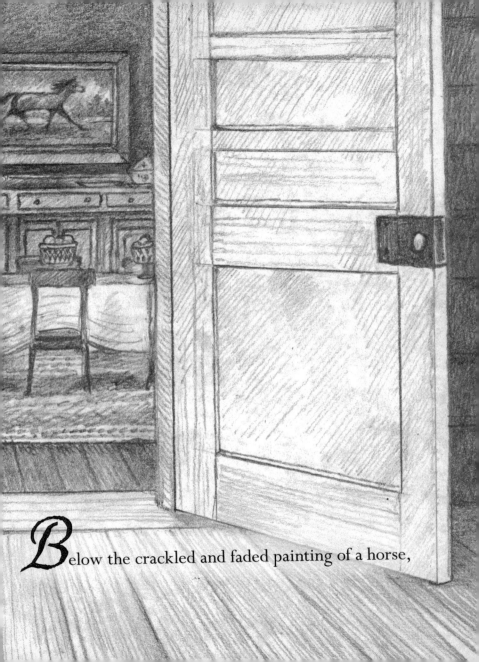

*B*elow the crackled and faded painting of a horse,

beneath the heavy sideboard,

under the worn carpet

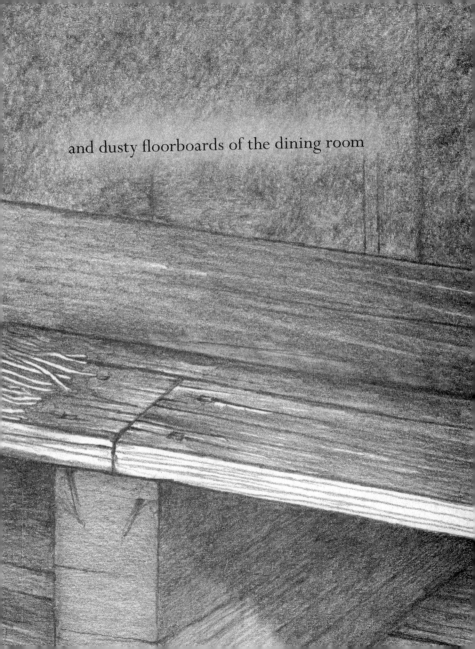

and dusty floorboards of the dining room

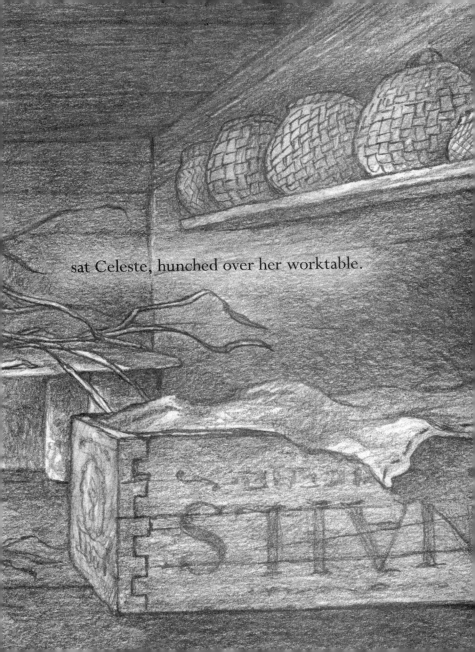

sat Celeste, hunched over her worktable.

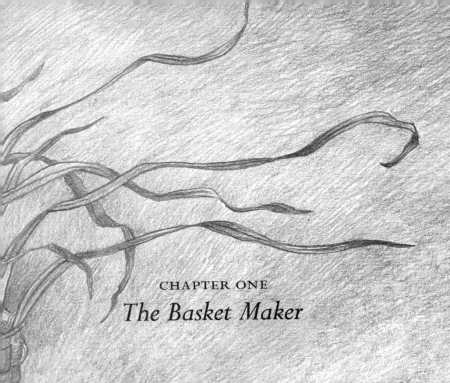

CHAPTER ONE
The Basket Maker

She was weaving a basket from blades of dried grasses. Above her head was a shelf full of the baskets she had made, some with dried wild-flowers or colored threads woven into them. Several had long shoulder straps, which made the baskets perfect for carrying bits of food or scraps of cloth. All of the baskets were skillfully made, with perfect knots and minuscule braids and weaving so tight the baskets could hold several thimblefuls of water or honey.

Celeste's newest basket was going to be of a design she hadn't tried before, with a side pocket and a fold-over flap to keep things from spilling out. Her nook was dim, but Celeste was used to it. From her pile of dried grasses she pulled another long blade and, using her teeth and nimble fingers, began twisting and weaving.

"Over, under, around, through, left over right . . ." said Celeste to herself as the grasses sang. The blades smelled sweetly of sunshine, of summertime.

As she wove them together she pondered over where the grasses may have grown. She had nearly forgotten what a sunny day was like. She spent her time under the floorboards, or upstairs in the dining room, furtively darting about in the shadows, searching for bits of food, plucking strands of horsehair from the dining-room chairs' seat cushions, or searching for bits of grass that had been tracked into the house on the shoes of humans. And always at night.

And lately Celeste had been finding something else on her expeditions upstairs: feathers. This was something new; she had never seen any before. Some were as small as her ear; others, long and pointy. Some were soft brown, others vivid green, still others brilliant blue and white. More often than not, after a venture to the dining room or crossing the hallway, she would return with a feather.

Finally, her paws a bit numb, Celeste tied off the last knot and sat back to examine the completed basket. "Goes quickly, once you have a rhythm going," she mused.

Her nose twitched, and she brushed dust from her whiskers.

She heard the deep gong of the dining-room clock resonate through the floorboards above her head.

Then she heard a rustling sound, and she glanced nervously down into the darkness of the tunnel between the musty floor joists.

Two gray rats emerged from the shadows and crowded into Celeste's nook.

No, it wasn't living in the darkness under the floorboards that Celeste minded. But these two, they were a different story.

CHAPTER TWO
Illianna and Trixie

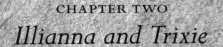

T he first rat, Illianna, had small, narrow-set eyes like a pair of black pepper-corns and a tongue like a lancet.

"Honestly, Celeste, another of your precious baskets?" she hissed. "Don't you have anything better to do than this silly pastime?" She brushed the remaining grasses off the table, then slumped in a chair.

The other rat, Trixie, began pilfering Celeste's food stores, searching through her baskets, helping herself. Celeste felt defenseless against the two marauders, who frequently bullied their way into her nook, ransacking and filching.

"Hmm . . . bread crust . . . more bread crusts . . ." Trixie said, her raspy voice wheezing between bites. "This bread is moldy! Where're the good bits, missy?"

"Um . . . what good bits, Trixie?"

"*What good bits, Trixie?*" In an instant the rat whirled around and nipped Celeste on the back. Celeste squealed. The pain was sudden and intense.

"You know what good bits!" Trixie screeched. "The really tasty bits . . . the bacon scraps and the sausage bits and the biscuit pieces. . . . You've hidden them from us, haven't you?"

"N-n-no, honestly," Celeste stammered.

"Try looking in her bed." Illianna squinted at her.

Trixie yanked the oily scrap of rag off Celeste's bed.

"Nothing!" she hollered. "There's nothing here! Well, then, you'd better get to it, missy. Take one of those baskets to the dining room and bring back something good. And mind you. No eating along the way! I'll smell your breath when you get back just to make sure."

"But I hear humans in the dining room. . . . It's still early yet."

"Well, I'm hungry!" Trixie snapped, and she made a sudden move, as though she were about to bite Celeste again.

"Me, too," Illianna chimed in. "Just keep to the shadows. Keep track of where the food is falling. And watch out for the cat."

Celeste obeyed the two rats. She knew if she didn't, the shoving and biting and insults and bullying would only increase. She skittered down the dark passage.

CHAPTER THREE
Mr. Audubon

Celeste sat in the shadows beneath the sideboard, listening and watching. She was worried about being seen, even a glimpse. Once she had clumsily let her tail protrude from the shadows, and a lady had screamed and dropped a dish. She wouldn't let that happen again.

She watched for the cat, a silent mass of gray fur that roamed the dining room. She saw five sets of shoes around the dining-room table. This meant that there were guests dining.

Two pairs belonged to the ladies of the house; she had seen them before and knew them well,

remembering their silk shoes beneath the rustling skirts and petticoats.

Another pair of shoes at the head of the table belonged to the master of the house. Celeste had seen him before, too. He had a fuzzy set of graying whiskers on each cheek and a red nose. Celeste noticed a napkin fall as he scooted his chair back and stood up.

"And now, Mr. Audubon," he said. "May I formally welcome you and your young assistant to Oakley Plantation and wish you a happy stay here." There was a clinking of glasses.

"*Merci* . . . ah, thank you, Monsieur Pirrie," boomed another deep voice. "Both Joseph and I are so very grateful for your hospitality. Your good wife, Madame Pirrie, is a most charming hostess. And your daughter, Miss Eliza, is a delight; I look forward to instructing her in the art of dancing, of drawing, and of painting. She looks to be someone . . . mmm . . . light on her toes? And she is now at the age to have dancing

with many *beaux*,
yes? Outgrown the
dolls, yes? I have the
latest gavottes and cotillions
from Paris for her to learn."

"Excellent, Audubon," said Mr. Pirrie. "That
sounds fine, mighty fine. I can't have my daughter
right on the verge of bein' courted by every buck in

the parish and not knowin' the proper way to dance. That Mr. Bradford over at Bayou Sara has taken on a fancy teacher for his daughters, and I won't give Liza anything less. I'll leave you in charge of all the drawin' and the dance steps."

"Thank you, *monsieur.*"

"And I understand that you'll be studyin' the birds around here? And paintin' their pictures?"

"Their portraits, *monsieur.* Yes, I will be collecting specimens of as many different species as I possibly can when not instructing Miss Eliza here. It is my intent to paint the portraits of every single species of bird in North America. And to paint the birds in their natural surroundings, and as lifelike as possible."

"Quite an undertaking!"

"Yes, it is indeed. And this evening I have brought along an example of what I am trying to achieve." He held up the large sheet of paper. "*Voilà* . . . a canvas-back duck."

Celeste could see a painting of a beautiful bird.

"Very nice, very nice indeed, Audubon," said Mr. Pirrie.

"It's quite large," commented Mrs. Pirrie.

"Yes, it is. It is life-size. I have much to do. It may take many, many months. My assistant here, Monsieur Joseph, is but a lad but is quite capable as an artist himself. He will be helping me with backgrounds perhaps, yes, Joseph?"

Celeste heard another voice, younger and softer. Still keeping to the shadows, she very carefully peeked up at the table.

"Yes, sir," the boy answered. He looked much younger than the other men. His hair was the color of a chestnut, and his face was smooth. His eyes were wide and pale blue; Celeste noticed something melancholy in them.

"Parents alive, son?" Mr. Pirrie asked.

"Yes, sir. In Cincinnati, sir," Joseph replied.

"Cincinnati? That's quite a ways from here . . . several weeks' journey! You're a long way from home, young fella."

Celeste watched Joseph as he ate. *That explains the lost look on his face,* she thought. *He's a long way from home. And lonely, too.*

"Monsieur Joseph has been a student of mine," Audubon explained. "The training and experience he receives as my assistant is invaluable. His mama and papa see that he has talent; he may at some point be quite capable at the botanicals."

"Botanicals, eh? That's plants and such, am I right?"

"Yes, sir," said Joseph. "Mr. Pirrie, I noticed that you have several magnificent magnolia trees in your yard . . . in full bloom. I've never seen such beautiful trees. And some outstanding specimens of tulip poplar, as well. Perhaps we can use those in our paintings?"

Mr. Pirrie looked pleased. "That'd be fine, son, just fine," he said.

The conversation turned to the weather, to the crops, and to horses as Celeste watched carefully for crumbs dropping to the carpet. Eventually, the candles and oil lamps were snuffed out for the evening. The dining room was dark and silent. Celeste prepared to venture out from beneath the sideboard to gather the remains of the meal.

CHAPTER FOUR

A Sudden Departure

C eleste felt a shove as Illianna and Trixie suddenly
appeared behind her.

"Where've you been?" Illianna whispered. "We're

practically starving, and you're here dawdling. I tell you, Trix, if you want something done right, you have to do it yourself." She sniffed the air. "Mmm. Something smells good." Her nose told her that with guests in the house, the spoils under the table were improving; and she was anxious to take advantage of things and sample every morsel.

She turned to Celeste. "You wait here," she said. "I don't want you getting all the good pieces first. Keep an eye out for the cat. Come along, Trix!"

The two shadows paused beneath the sideboard. Their noses waved back and forth as they studied the field of carpet and the forest of table and chair legs. They listened. Except for the ticking of the hallway clock, the only thing they heard was the galloping of their own heartbeats.

Trixie's nose sniffed the air. "That's piecrust," she whispered.

"Yes, indeedy, it is," replied Illianna.

"And is that spoon bread?"

"Last one there is a rotten egg!"

"Don't make me drool!"

And the two rats scampered out from under the

sideboard, carefully hugging the wall, following their noses to the broken piece of fallen piecrust.

No one saw the cat, seated on the needlepoint cushion of a dining-room chair, as it suddenly stop licking between two back toes. It peered into the shadows, pupils darkening, eyes as wide as those of an owl on a moonless night, watching the two shapes scurrying

along the baseboard. It raised its rear haunches slightly, careful to use only the necessary muscles, with only barely detectable movement. No blinking of the eyes, or flicking of the ears. No twitch of the tail.

The shadows made a sharp turn, away from the wall and straight to the table.

The cat grinned. Its back feet shifted ever so slightly, tensed and ready to pounce.

Illianna, whose favorite thing was day-old piecrust, suddenly stopped. "Wait!" She sniffed again. "That's piecrust . . . and something else."

A moment too late.

There was a ripping sound of claws on carpet as the two rats split paths, Trixie racing hysterically toward the front screen door and Illianna attempting

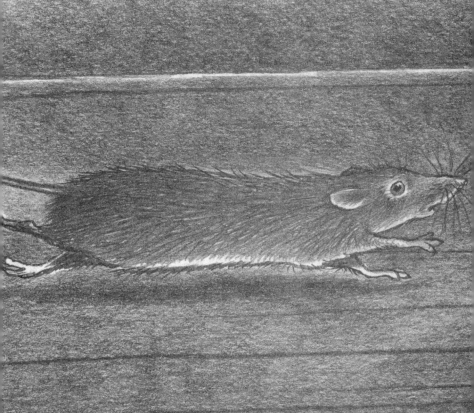

to rapidly circle back to safety under the sideboard.

But in an instant the cat predicted Illianna's turn and cut her off. There came a terrible, frantic, high-

pitched squeak for help, then a sound like wet fingers on a candle flame.

Frozen under the sideboard, Celeste squeaked in horror.

"Illianna!"

The cat ignored Celeste's piteous cry. Trixie, in a
frenzy, scrambled and wiggled through a crack under
the screen door and ran out into the dark evening.

Except for the soft ticking of the hallway clock, the dining room was again quiet, though Celeste's head echoed with the sound of Illianna's death cry.

She was alone.

CHAPTER FIVE

A Narrow Escape

Celeste checked her food stores. She had exactly two pumpkin seeds; the end of a small, shriveled sweet potato; half of a black walnut. Soon she would need to search for food.

And now that the cat knew her hiding place, foraging had become nearly impossible. One night she had started out only to find the hole completely blocked by a large pink nose and a set of black whiskers. The cat stealthily patrolled the edge of the dining-room carpet each night, leaving Celeste little chance to make forays from beneath the floorboards.

The next night she decided to start off again, this

time hoping that the cat would not be an obstacle. She chose her best basket, slinging it over her shoulder.

She poked her nose into the great space of the dining room and sniffed. The air smelled of candle wax, smoke, and the stale remains of a meal. There was also a faint odor of cat. Her ears flicked nervously as she crept along the edge of the carpet.

She followed her nose as it searched the crevices between floorboards and the fibers of the carpet for morsels of food. Her eyes could see all around her, except for directly behind her head. She listened for the smallest of sounds.

The clock ticked.

She stopped. Her nose found a small, dried lima bean. Tossing it into her shoulder basket, she moved on.

She came upon a feather, soft and white, dotted with gray spots. She packed it next to the bean.

Suddenly, all the soft hairs on the back of her neck

stood straight up, and her whiskers twitched. Her pupils widened. She froze in place.

Through the gray gloom at the distant end of the dining room, between her and the hole, she saw two large, yellow-green eyes. And the two eyes saw her.

She set off toward the hallway as though she was flying low, a tawny-colored blur. She careened into the hall, her legs skittering across the polished wood like drops of water on a hot skillet. She heard the scramble of claws on wood behind her and knew the cat was just one large lunge away.

Though the light was dim, Celeste could see just ahead a high tower with carved designs running up it. She had just enough time, she hoped, and just enough strength left to make it to the tower.

With any luck

she could use the carved leaves and vines to climb it.

And with any more luck the cat wouldn't be able to.

She sprang to the newel post in a leap that covered many floorboards. Her tiny claws found the minuscule crevices and notches in the wood and clung to them. She zipped up the tower in a panic of energy.

The cat was seconds behind but slid sideways on the polished floor, giving Celeste a hairbreadth advantage.

As the mouse scrambled to the top, the cat reached the bottom, leaping up in a furious attempt to snag Celeste. But Celeste was high enough, and the newel post was polished to a gleam. The cat stretched its claws, slipped, and missed.

It sat at the bottom, unmoving, staring up intently at Celeste. The hallway clock nearby boomed the hour: four.

From her vantage point, Celeste could see through

the doorway into the dining room to the sideboard. The sideboard now meant safety, and home.

The cat, a large cloud of dark fur, bored but not defeated, drifted silently into the dining room. It finally settled on its haunches, directly in front of the mouse hole. It seemed to know that Celeste would have to return at some point. With a sickening realization, Celeste saw that now there was no turning back: The cat was blocking the opening to her home. She felt small and exposed, the hallway around her huge and looming and foreign. Her throat constricted and she choked, thinking of her quiet, dark nook below the floorboards, of her warm matchbox and scrap of oily rag. Even the belittling comments and piercing squeaks of Illianna and Trixie seemed almost comforting now.

To inch her way back down the newel post meant certain death. It seemed the only way to go was up.

CHAPTER SIX
A New Nest

Celeste swallowed the lump in her throat and took a deep breath, as deep as a little mouse could take. She turned, her eyes following the railing up, up, up into the shadows, and started to climb. Her little claws clinging, she scaled the slope higher and higher until the hallway below her looked distant and foreign. Never in her life had Celeste been so high or felt so dizzy, or so exhilarated. She had to pause about halfway up, a bit out of breath. She glanced down. A flashing sense of vertigo filled her, and her ears blazed pink with a rush of blood. She felt enormously tiny in the cavernous hallway.

But she began to notice things that she had not seen before. There was the top of the tall, looming hallway clock. She had never known there was a

painting of the
sun and moon on
its face. The hanging
ceiling fixture, seen up close,
had tiny figures and wrought-
iron vines on it that she had not been
able to spot before. And the carpet runner,
viewed from such a distance, now revealed a pattern of lines and flowers.

"What a palace I've lived in!" whispered Celeste.

She spent a moment looking at the world from this
new perspective. The railing sloped up, beckoning her
on. She kept climbing.

She climbed until the handrail dead-ended abruptly
at a wall. By now it was nearly dawn, and the basket
sagged heavily, and her shoulder ached. There was no
sign of the cat.

She partly slid, partly climbed down to the floor.

Where to now? She had never been directionless

before. It was a
strange and uncom-
fortable feeling to have
nowhere to go.

The soft light of early morning

crept from beneath a door. Celeste scurried cautiously down the hallway and, sniffing anxiously, peered under the door.

She was looking into a small room. It had one window. The window sash was raised, and Celeste could hear birds singing as dawn awakened the garden outside. Under the window stood a small desk, which was covered with stacks of paper. Several jars of water lined the desk, each holding the stalks of a variety of plants.

An old shirt hung on a nail in the door. On top of a tall armoire was an empty cage. Tacked on the wall Celeste saw a series of small paintings, each one of a plant or an insect.

A small, low cot faced the window.

The dark recesses under the cot looked quiet and undisturbed, covered with a layer of dust. A leather boot lay on its side.

Celeste was completely exhausted; the night had been a long one.

The old boot looked inviting enough, although as

Celeste crawled into the toe, she saw it was a little dark and stuffy, and it smelled of human perspiration. But the space fit her perfectly; she even imagined herself inside one of her baskets, in the domed darkness. And she felt protected; should the cat ever roam the upstairs rooms, its claws couldn't reach deep enough into the boot.

But it needed sprucing up, and Celeste needed a bed. Cautiously exploring the room, she found several dried leaves that had fallen to the floor from the plants on the desk. She stuffed them into the toe of the boot. To these she added chewed bits of paper from several sheets she had nibbled through. Her prize find was an old woolen sock; she dragged the whole thing across the room with her teeth, then nibbled and unraveled it until she had made a satisfactory nest.

She liked her new home. "Well, I guess 'cozy' is a word for it," Celeste told herself. She closed her eyes and fell asleep.

CHAPTER SEVEN
Rescue by Dash

Her basket, unfortunately, held but one lima bean. The next night she decided that as much as she dreaded the search, she needed to find food.

She slung the basket over her shoulder and started out. It was a full night's journey down the flight of stairs and back up again. Hopefully, the return trip would be laden with spoils from the dining room.

She reached the main hallway and then lightly

scampered to the dining room. She scanned the carpet, ears flicking in all directions, straining in the still air for any unusual sounds. The hallway clock chimed. Twelve gongs.

Celeste's nose detected a piece of fatback over by a chair leg, and her basket began to fill. A minuscule scrap of sausage lay hidden under the folds of a linen napkin, along with several nut meats hidden among some cracked pecan shells. Seven watermelon seeds were scattered across the carpet. She gathered them all, stuffing them into her basket.

She raced back to the shadow of the sideboard to catch her breath. She hesitated, then darted to the hole; one of the baskets she had left behind would be useful now.

She raced down the tunnel to her old home.

The matchbox bed sat undisturbed. Her baskets lay around the room just as before. She grabbed one of the large, sturdier ones and stuffed it quickly with dried grasses, strands of horsehair, and a few feathers from her collection. She glanced once more around the little room. It looked crowded, dark, dusty, musty. Memories of life here seemed stale and backward now. She was excited about her new home in the toe of the boot. After a moment she headed out.

Back in the dining room, the umber underside of the table loomed above her like a starless night sky. She quickly covered the area at the head of the table, usually the more bountiful end. Here she found several more morsels: a crusty fragment of a baguette, complete with a tiny dab of butter; a slice of pickled okra; a bit of cheese. *The master of the house is a messy eater,* Celeste thought as she gathered a dozen bread crumbs, a burned crust of spoon bread, a greasy scrap of goose skin, and a raisin. She nibbled at a fallen dab of plum marmalade for energy. She raced to the hall doorway.

The baskets were full, and heavy. She paused to

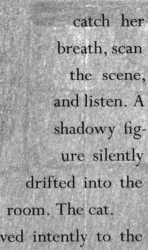

catch her breath, scan the scene, and listen. A shadowy figure silently drifted into the room. The cat.

It moved intently to the spot where the marmalade had been sticking to the carpet. It sniffed the area, its nose dipping and rising slowly several times while its pupils widened.

Celeste took a deep, deep breath, then raced toward the stairs.

The cat saw movement and tore across the carpet. Celeste heard the cat's breath right behind her and squealed in terror.

Suddenly there was the sound of the front door opening and human footsteps walking into the house. The sound of more claws spattered across the floorboards as a brown dog, as big as a dining-room chair, came tearing around the corner from the parlor. Barking and braying, it headed straight for the cat.

The cat stopped dead in its tracks. Then, turning blindly in panic, it ran straight into a corner by the clock, the dog following closely behind.

Celeste never stopped. She reached the newel post in less than a second and scurried up it as fast as she could. The baskets slowed her down; but with the cat distracted by the giant dog, she made it safely to the top.

Several doors opened upstairs, and heads peered over the stair rail into the darkness.

A gruff voice yelled from the top of the stairs: "Audubon! Blast it, can't you keep that dog of yours quiet?"

"Dash!" reprimanded a voice from the parlor. "Quiet,

you! You'll wake the dead! Dash! Quiet, I say!"

"What's going on down there, anyway?"

"*Pardonnez-moi*, Monsieur Pirrie. It won't happen again. Monsieur Joseph and I have just returned from our hunting trip. My apologies. Dash! Come!"

The dog obediently sauntered back into the parlor, with a backward glance at the glaring cat. Footsteps moved across the floor above, followed by bedroom doors slamming. A moment later Celeste watched as Audubon and Joseph retreated upstairs to their rooms, passing quietly by in the darkness. Then, silence.

Celeste waited for the house to settle down again before continuing her journey up. She slipped beneath the door and scurried to her boot. It had been a grueling night, but she had food that would last for days, if not weeks. Only when she had tucked away her baskets and was burrowing into her nest to go to sleep did she notice something strange: the sound of snoring coming from the cot above her head.

CHAPTER EIGHT
Joseph

The sun was changing the room from gray to gold when Celeste awoke to the creaking of the rope mattress just inches away. She peeked out of her boot and saw a young man pad across the room. She noticed the wave of chestnut hair. She recognized him. It was Joseph, Mr. Audubon's helper.

He was at the armoire, wearing a linen shirt, which was stained with what looked like paint or ink, and holding a leather boot in one hand. He was searching for something.

Then he was on his knees, scanning the floor.

He sat back, scratching his head. "Now where is

that other one?" he said, pulling on one boot.

Celeste suddenly realized what he was looking for. She cowered deep inside the boot and blinked.

That's when Joseph finished putting on one boot, and then began his search again. He swung around toward the bed.

Celeste felt her stomach sink as the boot was lifted. Her claws gripped the inside of the leather. In an instant there was complete darkness as Joseph's toes were thrust in, right toward Celeste.

She squealed in terror and, wriggling for all she was worth, tried to somehow escape the foot looming above her.

"Yeow! What the dickens?" yelled the boy, dropping the boot in surprise. It fell with a clunk, knocking

Celeste back down into the toe. Dazed, she peeked out. There was Joseph, looking in.

"Oh! A mouse!" said Joseph, smiling. He lifted Celeste carefully from the boot, cradling her with two hands.

Celeste was paralyzed, gripped around the chest with fear, unable to breathe much less jump or even move. Instinct told her to at least wiggle and squirm, but she could not. Her deep brown eyes could only stare at Joseph, whose own blue eyes showed that he meant no harm; they twinkled in bemusement.

"You're a pretty little thing," he said. "Maybe we can use you. Let's see . . . here's something that'll hold you."

Joseph took a small cage made of twigs from the shelf over the desk and nudged Celeste into it. "We made this for an oriole," he said, "but it'll work just right for you, too, Little One."

Celeste quickly scurried into a corner, making

herself as small as possible, glancing nervously about for an exit. There was none.

"Now I'll have company while Audubon is out," the boy said. "Lord knows it's lonely enough around here . . . lonely enough to talk to a mouse." He sat down to put on his other boot.

"What in the . . . ?"

He reached into the boot and pulled out a tangle of nibbled paper, leaves, and wool yarn. "My sock!"

He looked at Celeste and smiled. "Next time, ask my permission first," he said, tossing Celeste's nest through the open window. She let out a tiny cry when she thought of the food supplies—watermelon seeds . . . bread crumbs—that were now gone. And her baskets —a lot of hard work—lost.

She hadn't lived in her nest in the toe of the boot for long, but it had been home. Now it was out the window.

CHAPTER NINE

A Friend

Her heart beat furiously, like a million raindrops hitting a tin roof. The small cage had no places to hide in it, and Celeste felt exposed and vulnerable. Her body trembled, sickened with fear, as she watched Joseph putting on the other boot.

Why doesn't he eat me? she squeaked nervously.

But then Joseph sat down at his drawing desk. A large piece of paper lay stretched across the table right next to Celeste. She could see on it a penciled outline, the figure of a bird. Joseph began sketching what looked to be leaves or flowers in the background. He would sketch, then rub out his lines, then sketch again and again, only to rub out his lines each time.

He seemed frustrated, but spoke softly to Celeste as he worked.

"You're good company, you know that, Little One? I've been away from home so long I've just about forgotten what home is, but I know I miss it. Having you around is real nice."

He rubbed his eyes. "You know how long I've been gone from home? Nearly two years."

Celeste watched Joseph, who had stopped sketching. He was staring out the window, looking thoughtful. He seemed to have forgotten about her. Celeste searched again for an opening in the cage.

"Mr. Audubon asked me along on his trip as an assistant. . . . I had just turned thirteen," Joseph said. "I wasn't too keen on going. I remember when we started out on the river: The day was cool and bright, smell of pine and tar in the air; the little flatboat was new; and the men were busy on board, loading gear and supplies, packing everything. I felt I was in everyone's way, pretty useless. I had only brought along a few things: a shirt, some drawing supplies, a scarf. I stowed them in a nook belowdecks behind a barrel of hardtack."

Joseph reached between the twigs of the little cage and scratched Celeste under her chin. She froze, terrified. But Joseph's voice was soothing and eventoned.

He looked wistfully at Celeste and rubbed her tummy. Celeste closed her eyes and held her breath. *I'm really not much more than a mouthful!* she squeaked in panic, waiting for death. But Joseph seemed to ignore her squeaks and continued to talk.

"There was Ma, standing on the dock, wearing a black dress. She smiled at me, but I could see she'd been crying. She handed me a sack. 'Some biscuits and some ham,' she said. Someone yelled out, 'On board, lad!' and I jumped on."

Joseph again stared out the window, lost in a daydream.

"Our little boat pushed off, and I heard Ma say, 'Lord, be with him.' She got smaller and smaller, and that made me fill up with panic, like every nerve in my chest was being twisted. My throat got all pinched and tight, like I had swallowed a walnut whole. And I could feel the tears coming on, hot and fierce. Just about then Mr. Audubon put his hand on my shoulder. 'Prepare for high adventure, son!' he said."

Joseph turned from the window and looked at Celeste. "It's been adventure, that's for sure, Little One." He reached into the cage and gently took her out, cradling her in his hands, stroking her cheek. Celeste tried kicking and scrambling from his hands, but Joseph cupped her firmly. He found a peanut in his trousers pocket and gave it to her. She sniffed at it, perplexed, keeping her eyes on Joseph.

Then, cautiously, she began to nibble. It was

delicious. Celeste felt confused. It had been a long time since anyone had been kind to her. She had left her family's nest many months ago, and Illianna and Trixie had only given her blows to the ears and bites on the back.

Joseph continued. "The boat got into the current, and we started to make time. The dock and my ma disappeared around a bend in the river. A flock of geese flew over—there must have been hundreds of them—and the breeze picked up off the water. One of the men got out his fiddle and started playing a tune; and I started feeling better, not so homesick."

"It took us a while, but we finally made it down-river to New Orleans, and now here we are at Oakley Plantation. I tell you, Little One, seems like I've been working hard ever since, helping Mr. Audubon look for birds, then trying to paint backgrounds good enough. Sure would like to get home . . . but Ma says I can learn a lot from Mr. Audubon, that I can learn

a trade. Folks pay good money for beautiful paintings, you know. You're good company, Little One!"
He kissed Celeste lightly on the top of her head and
then slipped her into his shirt pocket. She wiggled at
first but soon sat quietly, waiting. The peanut in her
tummy had calmed her a bit.

Joseph went back to his work at his desk; she heard the sound of his pencil and eraser. But soon he became frustrated again. He jumped up from the table in exasperation.

"Mr. Audubon wants it perfect, and I can't do it!" he moaned. He peeked into his pocket. "Little mouse, what am I to do?"

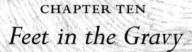

CHAPTER TEN
Feet in the Gravy

C eleste was getting accustomed to spending time nestled in the bottom of Joseph's shirt pocket. He kept her well supplied with peanuts and other goodies. Sometimes she liked to curl into a ball and sleep, lulled by the scratching of Joseph's pencils and his humming of tunes. But after several days

she found she was happiest when Joseph was working. She would poke her head out from his shirt pocket or perch on his shoulder and watch him sit for hours, staring at one of his jars of plants, and then try to make the plant come alive on paper.

"No! Not right!" he would mutter.

"Awful! The veins in this leaf are all wrong!"

"See how flat this looks? Terrible!"

Often Mr. Audubon would loom over Joseph as he worked.

"Composition, Joseph! Remember to balance the picture on the page!"

"Watch the watercolors, Joseph. Your greens are looking muddy."

"Why add this leaf? It does nothing for the picture."

Although Celeste could see how frustrated Joseph was, it was fascinating for her to watch him sketch, as he worked and reworked, over and over. To Celeste the drawings of the plants were beautiful, but Joseph never seemed satisfied. He would work late into the afternoon.

The dinner bell sounded from downstairs.

The table was set; food was being brought out from the summer kitchen.

Joseph sat at his usual place. "Good evening, Mr. Pirrie, Mrs. Pirrie," he said.

Mr. Pirrie was carving a roast. "Evenin', son. Got an appetite?"

"Yes, sir!"

Audubon entered with a flourish. His long hair was tied back with a ribbon, and he wore his best white linen shirt.

"Good evening, all," he said.

In Joseph's shirt pocket, Celeste's nose twitched. She was dreaming, but even in her dreams did things smell this good? She blinked several times before

realizing she was awake and the tantalizing scents were real, and close by. She poked her head out from Joseph's pocket.

This was a view of the dining-room table she had never seen. Several white tapers lit a brilliant array of colorful plates and dishes. Bowls and platters were piled high with mountains of food—incredible amounts that Celeste had never imagined. Silverware and crystal goblets sparkled. And wafting over everything like a delicious fog was the yummy scent of . . . was that roast beef? Succotash? Candied sweet potatoes? Hot rolls? Her eyes nearly bulged from their sockets.

"Yellow-jack fever is bad downcountry this summer," Mr. Pirrie said. "I heard the folks over at Parlange were hit mighty hard."

"At Parlange and also at other plantations," replied Audubon. "And of course New Orleans is in a bad state, so I understand,"

"Papa, will the yellow jack come up the river this far?" asked Eliza.

"Well, we're usually pretty safe here, Liza," her father replied. "President Monroe will send some militia to help quarantine the city."

Across the table, Mrs. Pirrie was helping herself from a dish of succotash.

"For pity's sake, let's not ruin dinner with talk about yellow jack," she said, passing the dish to Eliza. She happened to glance over at Joseph and stopped in midair. Her eyes got bigger, and one corner of her mouth dropped.

"Wh . . . wh . . . what's that?" she gasped. "Oh, no, no! A *mouse!*"

Celeste darted back down into the pocket, but the damage had been done.

The dish of succotash fell to the floor as Mrs. Pirrie leaped from the table and ran into the parlor, followed by wide-eyed Eliza.

"Mouse?" hollered Mr. Pirrie. "Where? There are no mice in this house."

In a panic, Celeste leaped from Joseph's pocket. Mr. Pirrie turned to see her racing to the edge of the table; and picking up a heavy serving ladle, he began swatting at Celeste, pounding the tablecloth and shattering a gravy boat. Celeste was

fast and miraculously maneuvered through an obstacle course of plates and silverware and repeated swats of the ladle, leaving behind tiny footprints of sweet potato and gravy. She leaped off the tablecloth to a chair, and then to the floor.

Right into the path of the cat.

Only inches away, the cat was too close to escape. Celeste closed her eyes tightly, preparing for the end. She had one second to think: *I only hope this is quick; I hope cats don't like to play with their food before they eat it.*

Suddenly she was enveloped in warmth and darkness. *This isn't so bad,* she thought. *The cat is merciful after all.*

Then she heard a voice whispering: "It's all right, Little One. Just stay still. But stay in my pocket this time!"

A second later she was deposited back into the familiar comfort of Joseph's shirt pocket. In an instant Celeste felt a measure of security and safety, tucked next to the familiar beating of Joseph's heart.

Audubon gave Joseph a look. Joseph understood immediately and hurriedly excused himself from the table, taking the stairs two at a time as he raced to his room.

"Don't ever show your face again, Little One!" he admonished. "At least, not at the dining table!" He put Celeste back in her small cage.

Her pulse was pounding. The world was an unpredictable place. Her little nook beneath the dining-room floorboards had been dark and musty, but it had been safe. She had never felt so strongly the need for a shelter, for a refuge, for home.

CHAPTER ELEVEN
A Portrait

The next afternoon Joseph stood by the bedroom window, hands in his pockets, listening to the pulsing drone of the cicadas in the magnolias outside. Downstairs he could hear Audubon

instructing Eliza in the parlor; they were in the middle of a dance lesson.

"And one. And two. And one. And . . . no, Miss Eliza, the left foot, not the right foot. Please, concentrate! You want the young men for miles around to come and admire your talents on the dance floor, yes?" Notes from the pianoforte began again.

Joseph had spent all day working on his botanical drawings; sheets of discarded paper, covered with attempted sketches, littered the floor.

He looked at Celeste. "Little One, I need inspiration!"

He pulled a cotton bandanna from his hip pocket, then folded and twisted it into a bowl-shaped nest for Celeste.

"Here you go," he said, sharpening a pencil with his pocketknife. "You just sit there and take a nap."

But Celeste couldn't sleep. She watched as Joseph started to sketch her. He began with a soft, arching

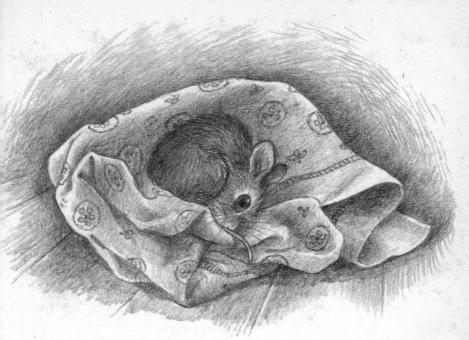

line: the contour of her back. Then a second line swept over the first, hinting at her tail.

"You've got such beautiful eyes, Little One," Joseph remarked. He studied her face and sketched the outline of her eyes and ears. Details followed: the white whiskers and pink nose, the tiny toes tucked under, soft and cream colored. With the side of his pencil he shaded in the background pattern of the bandanna and the tiny soft lines of her fur. He chose a softer, darker-leaded pencil and added still more details. Celeste watched as her eyes in the drawing became darker and more alive, the inner curves and shadows of her ears more prominent. Joseph took an eraser and touched certain places on the paper, creating highlights. The whole portrait took only minutes. Celeste could see that it was an exact likeness, with a warmth and spirit, and just enough details to show it was her, Celeste.

With a soft pencil Joseph signed his name along the edge of a shadow. "Hey!" He laughed. "You should sign your name, too, Little One. After all, you're the subject matter. And I can't think of a better subject!"

Using the blade of his knife, he shaved off some graphite dust from one of the softer pencil leads. He carefully gathered up Celeste, rubbed the bottom of one of her paws in the gray powder, and then gently pressed her paw to the paper, next to his own signature.

"Here," Joseph said. "This is for being a good model." He reached into his trousers pocket and fished out a peanut. "Your favorite!"

Celeste sat in the bandanna, contentedly nibbling the nut and gazing at her portrait.

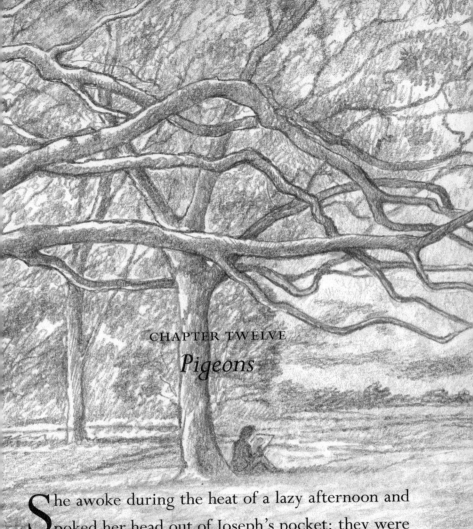

CHAPTER TWELVE

Pigeons

She awoke during the heat of a lazy afternoon and
poked her head out of Joseph's pocket; they were
in the shade of a magnolia, and Joseph was sketching.

Celeste casually looked to the north and saw a

massive cloud off in the distance. It spread low against the horizon, like a gray smudge. *A storm is coming*, Celeste thought, looking at the sky as it darkened and thickened.

"That's odd," she heard Joseph murmur to himself. He had noticed the same cloud. "No thunder or lightning flashes."

They sat watching the cloud swiftly approach. There was an eerie quality to it that Celeste couldn't quite put her paw on; it wasn't like the storms that she had seen come and go during the summer. There was no scent of rain pushing ahead of this cloud, no distant rumbling or shifting of air pressure. This cloud undulated and twisted. It spread and waved and rippled.

They heard yelling. Several men were racing across the yard, pointing and gesturing at the approaching cloud. "Here they come!" they shouted. A few of them were hauling logs and dead branches to an

open field one after another, making huge piles.

Still the cloud came closer.

The men dotted themselves across the field, and Celeste noted now that they were all carrying guns. "Get ready!" they called to one another.

And then suddenly the cloud was upon them.

Celeste looked
up, mesmerized, as it
became a living thing, the endless
puffs of cloud becoming enormous pulsing flocks
of birds, millions and millions of them. The flocks
stretched from horizon to horizon; Celeste gaped
openmouthed as she saw the entire sky filled with

layer upon layer of flapping wings. Their droppings pattered to the ground like a wet snow. Some flew near enough for her to see them clearly: graceful and strong, with rapid wing beats and long, pointy tails. Their feathers were a beautiful mossy gray with iridescent highlights that shimmered violet, green, and copper.

The beating of millions of wings created a rush of wind. The sound was astonishing, too—just like the wind from a thunderstorm.

Joseph seemed just as excited. "Hello! Hello!" he called up, waving at the huge

flock; and Celeste waved, too. The sight of it so exhilarated and amazed her, she wanted to be a part of it.

Then they heard the guns. They were firing from every direction, with blasts of buckshot that brought down several of the beautiful birds at once. Celeste saw hundreds, then thousands of them dropping from the sky every minute. The flock never changed its path. It kept moving in the same direction, seemingly never ending. A river of birds kept flowing overhead; wave after wave were shot, and the birds fell like hailstones.

Celeste smelled smoke. Looking down, she saw the piles of logs had been set afire. Thousands more of the birds were being choked as they flew through the smoke from the fires, and were dropping to the fields below. Their bodies were being collected and thrown onto wagons. The men were laughing and shouting, "We're going to eat good tonight!" and "Nothin' I love more than fried pigeon!"

Joseph had heard stories about the massive flocks of pigeons—the birds were called passenger pigeons—but he'd never witnessed one. And he'd seen hunting before, of course, but never as part of a wholesale slaughter like this. "I'm sickened, Little One," he said to Celeste.

Celeste burrowed down in the pocket and tried covering her ears; but still she could hear the sounds of the wings, and the shots, and the shouts.

The flock flew overhead all night and most of the following morning.

CHAPTER THIRTEEN
The River

Mr. Audubon's deep voice shouted from downstairs.

"Joseph! Let's go!"

Celeste could feel Joseph's heartbeat as she was jostled and swung back and forth in the shirt pocket.

She felt each jolt and bump as Joseph bolted down the stairs two at a time.

The front door slammed. She knew they had left the house but didn't know where they were heading. She heard the snorts and footsteps of several horses. After a while the rocking and swaying of the shirt pocket lulled her to sleep.

Later, when loud voices woke her, curiosity got the best of her. She hung her paw over the edge of the pocket, finding a grip in the buttonhole. She nosed her way under the pocket flap and saw that the men had tied the horses in the shade of some trees next to a river. Surrounding them was a forest of cane, tall grass that stretched up and up . . . taller even than the horses. A breeze was blowing in off the river, and the cane swayed and rustled like a million petticoats. *That grass would make quite a basket,* thought Celeste.

The men were soon boarding a small raft. Joseph and Mr. Audubon and some other men began poling

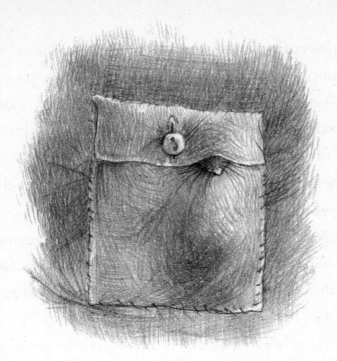

the craft out into the river. Dash was at the front of the boat, wagging her tail and looking excited. A large expanse of water opened out in front of them, stretching for nearly as far as Celeste could see. Huge trees, some larger than a plantation house, lined the river on each side.

Thousands of birds—some dark, some light, some

long necked, some short necked, but thousands of them—floated in groups, forming giant carpets on the water. Some chased and skittered and paddled after one another or dabbled their bills across the surface of the water. Some sat and busily preened their feathers; others napped contentedly in the sun. The air was filled with the din of quacks and honks and whistles. Above, hundreds and hundreds more were cascading from the skies, angling their wings and tails and dropping, splashing onto the surface of the river with feet braced for a water landing.

Celeste was thrilled. The breeze off the river was fresh and exhilarating, the clamor and activity on the water exciting. She gripped Joseph's buttonhole tightly, feeling strangely proud to be in partnership with him on such a day full of possibilities. She was on a real adventure.

After poling some distance out into the river, she noticed the men were busying themselves with their guns. She smelled something new . . . something acrid and pungent and biting in her nostrils. Her whiskers twitched with apprehension.

The flatboat approached a flock of ducks. Celeste could plainly see the faces and the feather patterns of the closest ones. Suddenly, in less time than it takes to blink, she heard an enormous *CRACK*. Celeste squealed and burrowed deep into the shirt pocket just as another blast sounded.

"Got 'im!" she heard one of the men yell. "Me, too!" yelled another.

What are they doing? wondered Celeste. She was shaking and wild-eyed at the bottom of the pocket.

She poked her head out again, and was immediately sorry that she had. Joseph and Mr. Audubon were pulling a dozen or so birds out of the water—the same birds with the beautiful feather patterns that she had been admiring moments before. The birds' bodies hung limp, drooped and lifeless. Dash was frantic, barking and sniffing. The remaining flocks of birds had lifted from the water with a roar of wings and were flying in chaotic zigzags down the river.

"Some good specimens, Joseph," Mr. Audubon was saying as they headed back to the shoreline. "This teal is nearly perfect. The rest . . . well, fellows, it looks like roast duck for dinner!"

He tossed the teal to Joseph.

"Hold its head up," he said. "And its wings. Quickly, while it's still warm."

Joseph held the duck for a moment, cradling its soft body. The breast feathers were still damp from the river, and Joseph could sense the warmth of its body on his fingers. He pulled the wings up with one hand, supporting the head and neck with the other.

In a moment Audubon had pulled a large sheet of paper from his portfolio and had begun an outline of the "flying" teal. Joseph and the other men watched as Audubon added more and more details: contour feathers, spreading tail feathers, eyes, and bill.

But Celeste burrowed back down into the pocket. She had seen enough. There was no more excitement and thrill to the outing on the river. It seemed that all of Audubon's paintings started out this way. The birds were beautiful, alive, and then they were shot from the sky.

CHAPTER FOURTEEN
A Close One

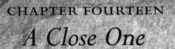

The men rode their horses slowly along the riverbank. It was tough going; they were hindered by the tangle of branches and roots from the huge trees.

Joseph put Celeste on the brim of his hat for part of the trip, a great vantage point for sightseeing. She perched,

gripping the hatband, fascinated by the scenery passing by. She had never seen such enormous trees. Their
limbs stretched up, covered in hanging moss, reaching

higher and higher until they ended in a blurred tangle. There were all sorts of strange and mysterious bird-calls and songs coming from them; Celeste felt tiny chills skitter across her skin.

Joseph's hand reached up to the brim, and Celeste gratefully grabbed at an offered walnut. "You all right up there?" he called.

Just then Mr. Audubon heard a certain call from high up in one of the huge cypress trees. He loaded his gun and fired, bringing down a large black-and-white bird with a scarlet crest of feathers on its head. The shot had only wounded it, damaging one wing; and the bird floundered around on the ground and in the cane. "That one we can use for a painting. We haven't got an ivory-billed yet," Audubon shouted.

The bird cried piteously and repeatedly tried to stab the hands of anyone who grabbed at it. Back on the hat brim, Celeste watched the cheerless scene; maybe she could help the poor bird, she thought, once

they got back to the plantation house.

"Haven't ever seen a woodpecker before, Little One?" Joseph asked, rubbing her behind the ears to calm her.

The men went out with their guns looking for wild turkey and other game. It was Joseph's job to walk through the cane, flushing out the birds. Stalks of cane towered way above Joseph's head and surrounded them like high walls of a small room. The dizzying tangle of waving green dwarfed them. They soon lost sight of the other men, and Celeste felt as if she was in another, strange world.

Suddenly they heard a shotgun

fire, and then a sound like an arrow hitting a haystack; and immediately Joseph keeled back into the cane. His hat, and Celeste, flew into the air and landed some distance away.

Celeste was disoriented and trembled in shock. The tall cypress trees and the thick cane towered over her. Evening was coming on, and darkness was spreading fast. She could see Joseph's body lying a little distance away. His head was red with blood; it covered his face and ear and trickled into a puddle under him. It took a moment for Celeste to get her bearings and realize what had happened.

The shot had hit Joseph in the head.

Celeste panicked. She frantically started climbing over the jumbled labyrinth of cane reeds, wanting desperately to get back to the safety of Joseph's pocket. She needed to know that he was all right.

The stalks of cane lay this way and that. Up she climbed, down she leaped, trying her best to grasp

and balance. When she got to a high spot she located where Joseph lay, checked her position, and then started out again. In a crazed burst of energy, she scrambled over the cane and reached Joseph in seconds.

"H-help! Help!" Joseph called out weakly.

Celeste let out her breath. She was relieved to hear him speak. She climbed up his arm, found his shirt pocket, and tunneled in.

Joseph smiled. He could feel the mouse over his heart.

"It's okay, Little One," he whispered. "It's just a scratch."

Audubon and the other men raced over to the boy and gathered him up. The stray shot had grazed his head just above his right ear. A surface wound only, but a messy one. His hair was matted and crusting over with dried blood.

One of the men washed out the wound and then tore off strips from an old saddle blanket, making bandages from it. "You know, Joseph, I could have swore you were the biggest wild turkey I ever did see!" he joked, and everyone laughed.

They started back to the plantation. And although

she was safely tucked in Joseph's pocket, Celeste
thought only of going home, someplace safe, wher-
ever that was.

CHAPTER FIFTEEN

The Ivory-Billed

Joseph hung his shirt on the door peg, with Celeste nestled in the pocket, and then collapsed on his cot, exhausted. Celeste could tell his head was throbbing, but the men had done a good job of cleaning and dressing the wound. She waited for his breathing to

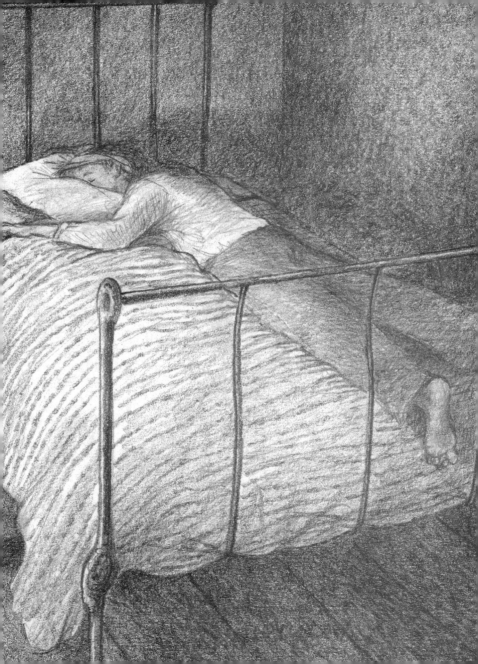

steady and slow, and finally he was asleep.

She watched the black-and-white bird, the wood-pecker. It scooted awkwardly around the room. Joseph had left it some grubs to eat, but the bird ignored them. It cried pathetically most of the night and hope-lessly hammered at anything wooden, reducing one of the chair legs to splinters.

The next morning Celeste saw it lying under the window listlessly. It seemed to have no fight left in it. Audubon took the bird and made sketches of it; but the drawings looked dull and lifeless, much like the woodpecker. Joseph took the bird outside to the garden, hoping that seeing the sky and trees would help. He laid the woodpecker under one of the mag-nolias, but it only stretched its neck out in the grass and stared up blankly. It again refused the grubs and worms that Joseph brought it. Celeste tried squeak-ing out encouragement from Joseph's pocket, but the woodpecker never responded.

Later that evening Celeste was perched in Joseph's pocket watching him sketch. The setting sun was streaming in through the bedroom window. They heard Audubon call out.

"Joseph! Fetch me some more pins!"

Dutifully, Joseph searched a wardrobe drawer for the pins.

As they entered Audubon's room, Celeste chittered in disbelief, then squeaked in horror. Audubon was carefully lifting the drooped and lifeless body of the ivory-billed woodpecker out of a canvas saddlebag. Its eyes were glazed over and cloudy. Its head hung down, jiggling like a knot at the end of a loose rope. The two wings, one broken and twisted, flopped forward and back as Audubon tried positioning the bird against a wooden board. Celeste could see that a small, dark purple streak of dried blood had oozed from the corner of its long, curved beak.

Celeste witnessed a change in Joseph's appearance.

His eyes were somber. His voice quivered a bit, stumbling for words.

"This doesn't seem right. . . ."

"What doesn't?"

"I don't know . . . the way we're doing this, the paintings."

"What about them?"

Celeste noticed Joseph's face getting red, and he was flustered as he spoke.

"You are looking to capture its life on paper, but by killing it first? By pinning it to a board?"

"I am painting their portraits; this is how they sit for me."

"It was so majestic up in that enormous cypress tree. . . ."

"There are plenty more woodpeckers where this one came from," Audubon retorted. "There were possibly dozens in the woods where I took this one. One bird less won't make any difference."

"Maybe we could—" Joseph offered.

"What?" Audubon shot back. "Do you want to hold the bird for me while it is still alive and have its bill slice through your hand?"

"Perhaps a cage—"

"No! A caged bird will sit like a caged bird. I want my specimens posed like I want to paint them.

Wings outstretched . . . as if they were alive!"

"But to kill them in order to make them look alive. . . ." Joseph shook his head.

Audubon glared at the boy, his eyes dark and angry. For a moment Celeste was afraid for Joseph, but Audubon just lowered his voice and held out his hand.

"The pins, Joseph."

Joseph handed the packet of pins to Audubon, who continued, "Your duty is to master the techniques of watercolor botanicals, not to question my handling of the bird specimens. I am preserving their beauty forever. If I could paint their portraits as well another way, I would. Now go!"

Joseph's face was red, his mouth rigid. He turned and strode down the hallway, leaving Audubon to sketch the pinned and trussed ivory-billed woodpecker.

He paused, thinking: *A landscape with no woodpeckers?* His life had seen lonely moments, and probably would again; but he couldn't imagine the loneliness of being the last of his own kind on Earth.

He thought about the ivory-billed; there were certainly other woodpeckers all along the river valley. But what if there was only one more? How would it spend the rest of its days? On an endless and futile search up and down the valley, looking to find another ivory-billed woodpecker?

As if sensing Joseph's melancholy thoughts, Celeste burrowed farther down in the shirt pocket.

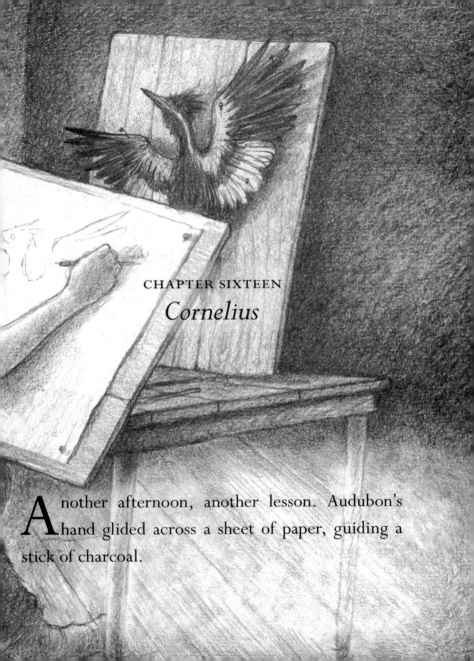

CHAPTER SIXTEEN
Cornelius

Another afternoon, another lesson. Audubon's hand glided across a sheet of paper, guiding a stick of charcoal.

"Observe," he commanded. The charcoal scratches eventually formed the outline of a crested head, a beak, and the posed body and wings of the ivory-billed.

Joseph sighed, trying to muster up interest in the lesson. To him, trying to listen to Audubon's instructions sometimes felt like pulling nails out of a plank. Instead of watching the charcoal, he stared out the window. He was wishing both he and Celeste were out exploring the woods around the plantation, looking for plant specimens.

Celeste's nose twitched as she watched from her pocket perch. The odor of putrefying flesh had begun to hang closely in the hot room, and flies hovered constantly around the bird.

They heard shouts below the bedroom window. Two young boys, the sons of one of the farmhands, were outside in the yard. The older one clutched something carefully to his chest.

"Mr. Joseph! We got something for you!" he cried

out. With excitement, he cautiously revealed a tiny portion of a feathered body. "It's a bird! Everybody says you wants to get birds. Well, we got one for you!"

Joseph raced outside and gingerly pulled back more of the old shirt. He saw a yellow bill and soft, creamy white breast feathers spotted with dark brown. "A wood thrush," he murmured. "Beautiful! Thanks, boys!"

"We found him in the lower barn. He must've flown in and couldn't get back out. It was easy catchin' him. He was scared."

"It was easy!" the younger boy agreed.

"Well, nice job, boys. This thrush will make for a beautiful painting." He gave the boys a coin from his pocket, and they ran off.

The little wooden cage soon had a new occupant. The panicky thrush, which probably had never been enclosed in anything smaller than the lower barn, now beat its wings against the twig bars, fluttering nervously about the cage. Thankfully, as night fell he became quiet.

The next morning, after Joseph had gone outside to wash, Celeste scrambled down the shirt to the floor and then carefully clawed her way up the brocaded drape and leaped to the tabletop.

"Hello!" she said to the thrush.

"Hello!" the thrush called back. His voice was low and silvery.

"May I introduce myself," began Celeste. "My name is Celeste, and I live in this house."

"I'm pleased to meet you," replied the thrush. "My friends call me Cornelius. . . . I'd be honored if you did the same."

"Thank you! Pleased to meet you, Cornelius."

"I live . . . well, I *did* live in the woods near here. I can't tell you how horrible it is to be trapped inside this cage after a lifetime of flying free. How good are you with escape plans, Celeste? I've worn myself silly trying to fly in between the bars of this cage, and lost some feathers in the process, as you can see." He looked up. "What about that little door?" Cornelius suggested. "Can you climb up there and unlatch it?"

Celeste squinted up at the cage door. "Hmm . . ." she said. "Just maybe . . ." She clawed up one of the bars of the cage to the latch. She tried undoing the wire clasp, but it was tightly twisted. "I might have

better luck just chewing through the bars," Celeste said. "It would take me a few days to make a hole big enough for you to squeeze through, but I'm sure I could do it."

Cornelius looked at her. "How did you come to live here?" he asked.

Celeste scampered down the side of the cage. No one had ever asked her that; she hadn't thought about her journey to the house at Oakley Plantation in a long time. She looked at Cornelius; his eyes were clear and thoughtful. Celeste could see that even though trapped in a cage, Cornelius was interested in his new friend.

"Well," she began, "I guess you could say I was rescued."

"Rescued? From what?"

Celeste thought back. There were details of her childhood she could barely recall; she remembered a nest made of grasses in a tangle of timothy hay and

wildflowers. She remembered three brothers and a sister, and a doting mother and father.

After a moment Celeste spoke. "My very first memory is of my mother. 'Francis, Silas, Beau, Louisa . . .' she would say, nudging my brothers and sister. 'Let Celeste in.' And I would wiggle and squirm until I had a spot at my mother's soft warm tummy to nurse.

"I remember all of us rolling and tumbling around our nest . . . a cozy dome of grass. There was a forest of grasses and weed stalks all around outside, and we'd explore it together. That's when I found I could twist and weave blades of grass together; my mother showed me how.

"Then one afternoon I was out gathering grasses. I shouldn't have been out of the nest, where the rest of my family was napping. It was a hot day. I heard human voices somewhere off in the field; they were singing. The voices got closer, and I heard another, strange, swooshing sound. As I raced back toward the nest, the tall, shady grasses were suddenly cut clean to the ground; there was this horrible glare and the heat of sunlight everywhere. . . . Our home had been sliced open by a long, curved blade. I saw the blade; it glinted in the sun and then swept back, slicing through the grasses over and over."

Cornelius hopped closer to the edge of the cage. "What happened then?"

"Well, I don't remember much after that, just lots of squeals and cries for help and frantic scrambling for safety. But after the humans had passed on, I was the only one left alive. I was wounded; I had been stepped on by one of the humans."

"But how did you end up here, in this house?"

"Nighttime came; I was still lying there in the drying hay. I remember it smelled so sweet. I was waiting to die, really. . . . I was so weak. I heard a rustling, and a groundhog lumbered up. I was too hurt and tired to say or do anything; but the groundhog—his name was Ellis—he carried me on his back, and brought me here to the house. He lived in a tunnel under the stone foundation. He gathered fresh

grasses and things to nibble on until I got better. I learned how to live in the big house from two rats; they showed me how to find food. Without my family, there didn't seem to be any reason to live in the fields again, so I decided to stay here for a while. That was many months ago. . . . I never left."

"What happened to Ellis?" Cornelius asked.

"I'm not sure; one day I heard shots from outside, and I never saw him again. I don't know if he was hurt or just chased away. He was a good friend."

She paused for a moment, thinking. She hadn't ever permitted herself to bring up memories of that day. It felt good to tell Cornelius.

"Thanks for listening," she said. "I didn't mean to go on and on. My plan now is to get you out of this cage. . . . But in the meantime, can I bring you anything? Something special that you like to eat perhaps?"

Cornelius replied excitedly. "Something like dogwood berries? The dogwood berries are beginning to ripen, and I haven't had one since last fall. I noticed a dogwood tree in the yard, just next to this house, with red and green berries all over it. Dogwood berries would be lovely!"

"That should be simple enough," said Celeste.

"You could do that?"

"I'll see what I can do. I can try finding some once it gets a little darker outside."

"Wonderful. Being in this cage is a nightmare!

You've given me . . . well . . . a little glimmer of hope."

The wood thrush then lifted his head and let loose a startlingly clear warble that resonated throughout the room. The beauty of it made Celeste's chest give a tiny heave; and she felt a pang, and an ache so intense that her heart skipped and trembled. She clutched at it with her paw.

The lilting birdsong ended, and the room was still.

"I don't know which I like better," Celeste whispered, "your beautiful song, or just after."

The thrush smiled.

"Do that for Joseph," Celeste stated firmly. "Sing just like that. Promise me."

Cornelius shrugged his wings, then nodded.

CHAPTER SEVENTEEN

Outside

The stagnant air sat unmoving around the plantation. The oppressive heat seemed even hotter because of the persistent drone of cicadas in the treetops. Celeste looked out over the garden from her vantage point on the bedroom windowsill. She could see a dark bank of clouds far off to the west, still miles away but moving toward the plantation. If she wanted to find Cornelius some dogwood berries—and she had said that she would try—she'd have to do it soon; she did not want to be caught out in a storm.

She remembered when Ellis once spoke of a tunnel, a little-used passage that led from under the floorboards through the stone foundation of the house to the outside beyond the cellar. Maybe she could use this passageway to locate the dogwood tree. She bid Cornelius good-bye and set off.

The early evening provided enough shadows to hide Celeste. From Joseph's room she warily made her way down the two flights of stairs and to the dining room without being discovered. She saw no sign of the cat; perhaps the heat of the day had sent it to doze on the front porch.

Her old home under the floorboards seemed even dustier and darker than she remembered. Her remaining baskets lay in a jumble. She picked the largest and strongest one, throwing it over her shoulder.

She checked all along the tunnel under the sideboard. Finally she discovered a small entryway. It led to a crevice between the cool stones of the house's foundation. Up ahead, she saw daylight.

She poked out her nose and then emerged from the house into a tangle of shrubbery, feeling thankful that she was hidden.

Her eyes widened at the scene around her. She suddenly realized how alone and vulnerable she was without the protection of Joseph's shirt pocket. The forest of plants, the sounds, even the red clay soil under her toes seemed foreign to her. Each of her senses prickled with excitement.

She looked up between the branches of an azalea bush. Steely gray cloud formations were now blocking what was left of a pink streak of sunset, and she heard deep rumblings of thunder. There were shouts near the barns and fields, warnings and commands: A storm was coming and all things needed to be secured. Celeste heard the whinnies of horses as they were hurried into the barn, along with wagons of cotton and flax.

The barn! Now to find the dogwood tree.

Her eyes moved from the barn to the split-rail fence that surrounded a pen, and she could see, even from this distance, a large hog lying there.

She hurried through the yard and across the lane to the pen.

The hog seemed to be asleep. Celeste climbed up onto one of the rails and called out.

"Hello!"

The hog woke up with a quick snort. He was enormous, with friendly, curious eyes.

"Hmm? Who's that?" he asked.

"Sorry to interrupt your nap," Celeste said, "but could you direct me to the nearest dogwood tree?"

"Dogwood? With the little red berries? Follow your nose! End of the fence there's a dogwood. Just stay on the fence rail and you're there!"

"Thank you! Thank you so much!" Celeste called out as her tiny paws scampered along the split rail. And indeed, ahead of her she saw a small tree laden with red fruit.

"Hey! Get inside!" she heard the hog grunt after her. "Storm's comin'!"

Now to find the dogwood tree.

She decided to turn right, and dodged around ivy vines and iris leaves, nearly bumping into a fat, brown toad.

"Hey, dearie! Where's the fire?" the toad croaked.

Celeste gulped. She had never seen anything that looked quite like this.

"Hello," she stammered. "I'm looking for a dogwood tree . . . but I'm not sure where it is. I can't get my bearings. . . . Do you know of any nearby?"

"Dogwood, eh?" answered the toad. "Yep. You're heading the wrong way. Turn around; head straight, all the way to the corner of the house. Can't miss it."

"Thank you very much!" Celeste turned and started off. She heard a rumble of thunder not far off as the storm started to blow in.

"Better be fast, dearie!" the toad called after her. "Storm's comin'! Feels like it's going to be a big one!"

The toad watched Celeste race away, then hopped into the protection of the ivy vines. "Yep," she croaked to herself. "Every bump on my skin can feel it. It's going to be a real big one!"

CHAPTER EIGHTEEN

The Storm

Celeste ran along the edge of the stone foundation, hurrying beneath an arching tunnel of
azalea and camellia bushes. At the corner of the pen
she arrived at last at the dogwood, branching low
to the ground and easily climbed. Not too high, but
at the ends of the branches, she saw red and green
berries.

Up she went, nimbly scrambling along a branch
until she came to ripening clusters of the dogwood
fruit. Immediately she began nibbling off berries and
stowing them in her basket.

Suddenly the thunder stopped rumbling and started crackling.

"Chew! Chew faster!" Celeste said to herself. Her jaw began to ache. By the time she had just a small bit of room left in her basket, the first drops of rain began to fall. Each as big as her ear, the drops fell from the black sky like spears. They pummeled her, nearly knocking her off the branch, nearly blinding her. Others struck her back and shoulders, drenching her fur. Then, with an eerie roar, the wind picked up and tossed the treetops.

The leaves around Celeste were flattened and beaten as the rain increased. Drops slashed at her face. Rivulets ran down the tree trunk and then gathered into streams and waterfalls.

What had been low rumbles of thunder churned into waves of crackling fury as lightning flashed in the sky. Trickles of rainwater on the ground quickly

became streams, then torrents, turning reddish brown with clay.

A crash of lightning hit so close by it seemed inches away, shaking and rattling windows of the house, and Celeste screamed in terror. In the brilliant flashes she could see rivers of water everywhere and a tangle of wet, flapping leaves. Disoriented and terrified, she floundered through the chaos, trying to find her way back down the branch.

The wind increased even more, rocking the tree and buffeting Celeste back and forth, rattling the roof of the barn, and blowing bits of leaves and debris into the sky like gunshot.

A particularly furious gust of wind whipped the branches of the small tree, and Celeste struggled to hang on. The basket of berries was ripped from her, and it flew away, lost in the swirling maelstrom. And then she finally lost her grip and was blown from the branch, out into the dark blast.

A moment later she was plunging into a whirlpool of brown-red water, leaves, sticks, and other debris. She kicked furiously and came to the surface, squeaking helplessly. The fast current grabbed her; and she bobbed up and down, gasping for air, paddling with her front paws and kicking with her hind feet. A large piece of bark struck her; and she clutched at it, throwing her body over it, clinging desperately. Heavy rain slashed and slammed into her face; and she choked and coughed on water and mud.

The road leading to the plantation had become a small but raging creek; and by the lightning flashes Celeste was terrified to see that she was being carried away from the lights of the house and out into the darkness.

She was chilled to her core and starting to shake.

The current got stronger. Water gushed in a torrent that carried off the little bark raft with Celeste, numb with cold, clinging to it.

After riding through a series of rapids and strong currents, the raft bumped into a muddy bank and slowed, then drifted against a sandy shoal and stopped. The heavy rain had stopped and was followed by a cold drizzle. Celeste's coat was soaked and caked with mud and sand. She shivered with uncontrollable spasms. All her strength was spent. As her mind turned to darkness, she sank into a deep sleep, her cold body wet and sagging over the curled piece of sycamore bark.

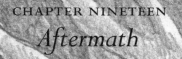

CHAPTER NINETEEN
Aftermath

The day dawned bright and clear. The sun was hot and brilliant, but the shade under the trees was cool. The storm during the night had washed away the dust of summertime, and now the sky was cobalt blue. Wet leaves were plastered against the trees and fences, houses and barns. Broken tree limbs littered lawns, and countless hollyhocks and sunflowers lay prostrate, blossoms stuck facedown in the mud.

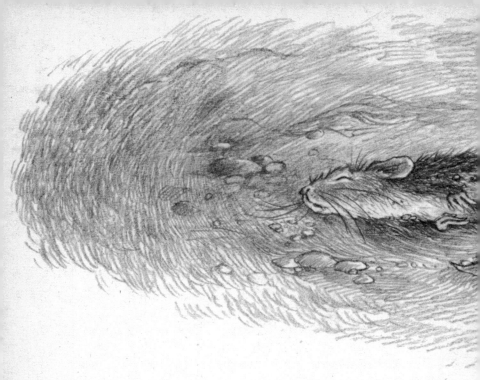

Roads were pitted with gravelly ruts that had been washed out by the raging torrents of the night before. Birds began singing again as a salute to those among them that had survived the storm.

Celeste blinked. She saw the sky, heard a cardinal and a mockingbird singing morning songs. She moved to sit up, but her body ached; her fur was stiff with

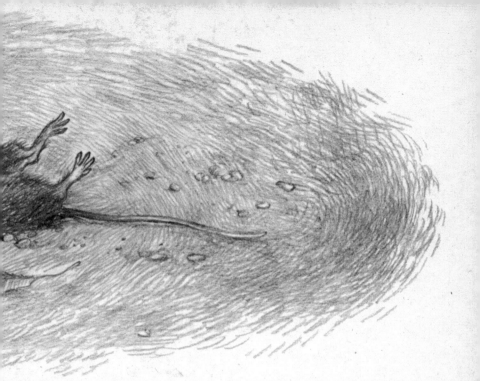

mud. In a cloudy blur of pain and weariness, she sank down again.

The first of the stars began to appear, bright and sharp against the clean sky. A catbird sang an evening song. The swollen creek had dwindled to a gurgling trickle. Still Celeste didn't wake from her dreamless sleep.

CHAPTER TWENTY
Lafayette

It was the dappled glow of the late-summer sun that finally revived Celeste, warming her body, soothing her aches.

She sat up and blinked, trying to take in her strange surroundings. Tall sycamore trees towered overhead, their roots twisted and arched and sculpted by the riverbank. A jungle of purple, yellow, and white wildflowers, most of them beaten down by the rainstorm, was being visited by scores of brightly colored butterflies. Celeste had never seen anything so dazzling.

But she paid little attention to the beauty of butterflies. She was starving. Every bit of her energy had been spent in surviving the storm. Glancing around, she found some soft grass blades and nibbled at those. She made her way along the sandy riverbank slowly; found jewelweed seeds, some wild cherries that had blown to the ground, and a small beetle; and quickly gobbled them down.

She was totally disoriented—which way was the plantation? Intuitively she figured she should head upstream, along the bank; but how far?

She was contemplating her next move when suddenly she was cast in shadow. An enormous bird swooped down at her, almost but not quite grabbing her with strong talons, and then landed with a flourish beside her. Celeste did a double flip in the air, landing on all fours, ready to race away. But the bird didn't attack; in fact, it looked at her curiously and asked a question: "Are you out of your cotton-pickin' mind? What are you doing way out here in the middle of the day? You should be under cover somewhere—somewhere safe and protected— 'cause something's going to want to eat a little tidbit like you, sweetheart!"

Celeste was so surprised she could barely say anything. "I . . . I . . ." she stammered.

"I understand perfectly, darlin'," the bird said. "You're lost, you're covered with dried mud, you look like a drowned rat, and I bet you're hungry enough to

eat a dead polecat. Am I right?"

Celeste couldn't help but giggle. "Yes! Do I really look like a drowned rat?"

"You do indeed, honey pie. You take a ride on a mighty big raindrop last night? That was a humdinger of a storm!"

Celeste smiled. She liked this big bird! He had huge, golden yellow eyes that twinkled and a sharp beak that smiled. His wing feathers were dark brown, his chest creamy white with tawny streaks and spots. There was something slightly amusing about him that made Celeste feel safe and happy at the same time.

He continued. "I was way, way up in the air; and I looked down and I said, 'Lafayette'——that's my name, sugar plum, Lafayette——well, anyways, I looked down and I said to myself I said, 'Self, now, that looks like somebody in trouble; that's what I think. I need to go check on that one, like any good osprey would do'; and I circled a couple of times and then swooped down, and here I am! Now, what I want to know is, are you in trouble or not?"

Celeste thought she'd better answer honestly. "Yes, I guess I am, Lafayette. I got swept up in the rainstorm last night, and the current carried me here. I don't know where I am!"

"Lost, huh?" Lafayette scrunched his face as he stretched out one wing, then the other. "Ooh! That feels good! Been flying all morning." He sighed.

"Your wings are amazing. . . . Is it fun to fly?" asked Celeste.

"Well," said the osprey, "I guess I never thought much about it. You're high up, of course, and so you can see quite a ways. It's quiet, and very green, because there's mile after mile of treetops—tall, tall sycamores—just the river and fields in between."

"Sounds lovely," murmured Celeste.

"Most of the time I spend sailing up and down the

river," the osprey continued. "I know every snag, every shallow, all the good trees to sit in. Up and down, up and down, miles and miles along the river."

"I live at the plantation, in the house. Do you know the plantation near here? I want to get home."

"Well, there's lots of plantations 'round these parts. Lots of 'em. You say you live in a plantation house?" He eyed Celeste doubtfully. "Well, well. Which one is yours?"

"It's a big house, with big magnolia trees around it. There are some barns, and horses; and a family lives there, and so do I."

"Hmm. You're a long way from home, that's for sure, dumplin'. The closest plantation is quite a ways. There's the big plantation beyond the cypress woods, and the big plantation out on past the bayou, and . . ." Lafayette continued talking, telling Celeste about his brother-in-law up the river and his second cousin once removed down the river . . . chattering away while Celeste was formulating an idea.

She interrupted him. "Um, Lafayette," she said. "Could you meet me right here at this very spot tomorrow, say right about sunup?"

"Why, sure, sweet potata. I can be here any time you say. But what for?"

"I want you to help me get home."

"Now, how do you figure I can do that? You gonna

hang on to my claws? Ride on my back? That's a little dangerous, don't you think?"

"I've got a plan, and I think it will work. Will you be here?"

"Yes, ma'am. I'll be here. You want to tell me what the plan is?"

"I think I'll surprise you, Lafayette!"

"Okeydokey, I like surprises. I can wait to hear about your mysterious little plan. And now that I know you're all right, will you pardon me while I continue on with my fishing trip?" With a series of strong flaps, he lifted into the air. "Toodle-oo!" he called from high above the sycamores. "Now, you be careful!"

Celeste was alone again.

CHAPTER TWENTY-ONE

The Gondola

First, Celeste went to the edge of the creek and took a long, cold bath, rinsing out the dried mud from her fur and whiskers. *"Brrr!* That was cold, but it feels good to be clean again!" she said, shaking off as much water as she could.

Then she set to work, finding a spot nearby under the protective cover of some thick weeds. She started by collecting dried grasses and weed stalks from the surrounding area, gathering big armfuls from the thick tussocks that were growing in abundance along the creek. She was delighted to find several strands of horse or cow hair, washed along the banks of the creek from some distant pasture upstream.

Emerald green dragonflies and cerulean dam-
selflies darted around her head as she worked. She
stopped briefly to nibble on more seeds.

She carefully laid out her supply of dried mate-
rial across the ground. She selected only the strongest
grasses, those without any insect damage or weak
stems or other flaws, and set them to one side.

Of the selected grass blades, she chose the two
thickest ones and, braiding them tightly around the
strands of horsehair, made a very strong length of
rope. Then she started weaving a large basket, bigger
than any she had made before, using strong blades of
grass and weaving them tightly and with extrastrong
knots. She took the rope and wove it into the basket,
interlacing it over and through as she created a large
gondola, big enough to hold a mouse, with a rope handle. Celeste thought of her mother as she worked. Her
mother would have been proud.

The moon rose, a pale rose-colored disk that

illuminated the jewelweed.

Before morning she had nearly finished. Scouting the sandy shoreline of the creek, she found several tiny white coquina shells with holes in them, and used them to decorate the sides of the basket. As a last touch, she added a red cardinal feather.

Celeste carefully dragged the basket to a little clearing in the weeds. She covered the basket with a sycamore leaf in preparation for Lafayette's return.

CHAPTER TWENTY-TWO
Lafayette Returns

Sure enough, just before dawn Celeste heard the osprey's high-pitched call as he wheeled and soared above the creek. She ran back and forth along the sandy bank until the osprey spotted her far below.

He circled and swooped and landed lightly, if awkwardly, on the narrow creek bank.

"Not much room for a landing," Lafayette joked. "How are things with my little sugar pie this morning?"

"Oh, I'm fine," answered Celeste. "But I do have a favor to ask of you."

"What's that, sugar plum?"

"Would you take me home now?" asked Celeste.

The osprey raised a brow.

"I don't weigh very much," she added.

Then he grinned. "Why sure, honey! But now, just how would you suggest I do that?"

With a flourish, Celeste pulled away the sycamore leaf and revealed the basket. There was the tightly woven gon-dola with its reinforced strap, complete with decorative shells and a cardinal feather.

"Holy catfish!" exclaimed Lafayette. "You've been busy! Is this your mysterious plan? It's *splendid*. . . .

Did you actually *make* this?" He picked up the basket gently with his beak, turning it around and admiring it from all sides.

Celeste blushed. No one had ever admired her work before. She hardly knew how to react.

"There's nothing to it, really. Usually the difficult part is getting the supplies, but there were plenty of grasses around here. After that it's a matter of the doing. I just do what my paws say to do."

"I admire those folks who are clever with their paws." The osprey sighed, studying the intricate basket. "I've always been so clumsy with my talons."

"I can't imagine you being clumsy at anything," said Celeste.

"Aw, go on!" Lafayette blushed. "I could never do what you can do. This basket is amazing! A work of art! And all by your lonesome? You're amazing, sugar pie! And you're thinking I can give you a ride in it?"

Celeste pointed to the two straps. "If you grab

here, and here, with your talons, I'm sure it's sturdy enough. And it's lightweight, too, so I wouldn't be much of a burden. Can we give it a try?"

"Absolutely! I'm game if you are. Afraid of heights?"

"Well, I don't know . . . yet!"

The morning air was cool and damp, and heavy dew covered every surface. Even in the predawn light Celeste could see that the entire world was blanketed in silvery droplets. The air was full of the scent of magnolia and jasmine blossoms. Celeste couldn't wait to try the gondola.

Lafayette's eyes glowed and his feathers were ruffled with anticipation as he maneuvered the basket. He carefully clasped its handle in his talons and lifted it with one foot. Celeste hopped into the gondola and gripped the rim tightly.

"Ready?" he called out.

"Ready!" she cheered.

CHAPTER TWENTY-THREE

Flight

With a few flaps of the osprey's powerful wings the basket lifted slightly. It dragged for a moment along the sandy shoal and then, in a flash, the ground dropped away as Lafayette soared upward. Celeste squealed as a sycamore loomed in front of them, then below them, then behind them as the two rose and wheeled in the air.

Celeste turned in her basket. The osprey's huge tail feathers fanned out in a striped pattern above her head.

Lafayette flapped over the creek in a widening arch, and Celeste could see the world getting bigger as they soared up. She saw that there were other creeks, and vast stretches of woods and fields, dotted with houses and barns, striped with fences and sandy roads.

"Hanging on tight?" the osprey shouted down to Celeste.

"Yes!" she chittered back. She clutched the rim of the basket, adrenaline racing through her tiny body. It seemed that all her strength and energy was spent clinging to the basket, but she desperately wanted to remember every detail of the flight.

The creek bank was soon far behind. She looked down, trying to find a familiar landmark, but didn't recognize anything. The distant fields and woods were deep green in the early-morning light, the air cool and misty as it flowed past Celeste's whiskers.

"Should I go back down?" called the osprey.

"No! This is wonderful!"

"Hold on! Now I want to take you for a real treat."

Lafayette banked his wings to the left and angled sharply.

"Eee!" Celeste squealed rapturously. "Do that again!" And the graceful bird dipped and swooped danger-ously close to the treetops.

"See that? The river!"—and he turned again, near-ing an expanse of water nearly a mile wide. The sun had just peeked above the tree line to the east, turning the water into a golden mirror dotted with hovering patches of peach-and-honey-colored mist. Hundreds and hundreds of ducks were careening along the shoreline in loose flocks.

The osprey dipped slightly as they neared an enormous sycamore tree along the riverbank; as the basket glided between its branches, they saw scores of

yellow, green, and orange parakeets.

"Hello, down there!" Celeste called to them.

"Hello!" they chattered and screeched back.

Lafayette continued up the river, alternately soaring just above the treetops and flapping just above the water's surface. Celeste breathed deeply, enjoying the sweet, musky smell of the river as the air rushed across her whiskers.

They headed toward an open part of the woods; Celeste could see that it seemed to be flooded with river water. The trees were different here, not like the thick stands of poplar or the spreading branches of the live oaks that grew in the yard of the plantation. These trees seemed to pop right out of the water. Their branches were festooned with long tresses of hanging moss.

She looked closer. Down along the banks of the dark water she could see long, rough-skinned creatures basking in patches of sunlight. One of them opened its huge mouth as they flew over and bellowed. Celeste could see rows of sharp teeth.

"Gators!" Lafayette hollered out, grinning. "Hold on tight! Don't want to drop you now!"

They flew above long-necked birds that lined and dotted the tree limbs by the thousands. As Lafayette and Celeste cleared the tree canopy they surprised the birds. The birds' necks and wings stretched out, and they squawked and croaked in a deafening cacophony. Celeste looked down as the entire flock took flight, flapping and swirling, brilliantly white in the morning sun.

Lafayette flew in

long, wide circles over the area, with Celeste scanning for anything familiar. Suddenly she shouted out. "There! Below! That's it, I'm sure! That's the big house!"

It was hard to recognize, because she had never seen the plantation house from this view; but the little bedroom window with the magnolia nearby was unmistakable. Lafayette circled down.

"I'm glad I've gotten you back before the sun was up too high or else someone would start shooting at me," the osprey called down. "More and more guns shooting into the air these days. . . . It's gotten so a bird isn't safe in his own backyard anymore!" The wings

stopped beating for a moment, and the bird glided and banked again, turning closer to the house.

The morning was brightening, and Celeste could see that the early activity of the plantation had begun: Horses were pulling wagons toward the rice and sugarcane fields, and smoke was rising from a few chimneys dotted across the landscape.

Celeste had another idea.

"Lafayette! Drop me at this dogwood tree for a minute, please!"

"What?"

"Just let me grab something before you leave me at the window."

Celeste quickly but carefully climbed out of the gondola and grabbed on to a branch of the dogwood tree. Lafayette hovered overhead. Finding a cluster of berries, she hurriedly chewed through the long stem. She grabbed the stem firmly before leaping back into the basket.

"Up to the window, the one on the left!" Celeste called out, and they flew to Joseph's windowsill.

The osprey hovered just above the windowsill as Celeste carefully leaped out again.

"I'll see you soon, sweet pea!" Lafayette called down.

"Thank you!" Celeste squeaked, as Lafayette dropped the basket on the sill. "For getting me home. And for the most wonderful time I've ever had!"

CHAPTER TWENTY-FOUR

A Homecoming, and Inspiration

Celeste hopped onto the desk and glanced around the room. She was ecstatic to be back in Joseph's room, where things looked and smelled and felt comforting. Her heart felt a twang when she saw Joseph's shirt hanging from its wooden peg. Cornelius was perched in the cage, head tucked under his wing, eyes closed. Celeste heard soft breathing coming from the cot, where she could see Joseph draped, sound asleep.

She squeaked up at the cage. "*Psst!* Cornelius!"

Cornelius opened one eye.

Celeste tried again. "It's me!"

Cornelius leaped up with a start, calling from his cage. "Well, look what the cat dragged in!" he chirped.

"Quiet! I don't want to wake anyone!"

Cornelius glanced over at the cot. "Hey," he whispered, "I've been worried sick! Where in the world have you been?"

"Well, it's quite a tale, involving lightning, wind, lots of rain, mud, almost drowning, and an osprey." Celeste sighed.

There was a creaking from the cot. Joseph was turning over in his sleep.

"Here, a present for you," whispered Celeste.

"Dogwood berries!" chirped the thrush. "You remembered!"

"Help me get this branch into your cage."

She poked one end of the branch into the cage, and Cornelius eagerly plucked several berries, gobbling them down two at a time.

Celeste whispered, "Now, pull! Pull your end!"

"Pull? Pull it where? What are you trying to do?" Cornelius asked.

"You'll see. Just keep pulling until I say stop!"

They pulled and pushed until the dogwood branch was in the cage. With one final shove, Celeste sank the chewed end into the brass water dish.

"Hey! That's my drinking water!" exclaimed Cornelius.

"Keep your voice down! Now, listen. The next time Joseph starts to sketch, sit right about here," said Celeste, pointing to a spot on the branch. "And it wouldn't hurt if you sang something."

"Well, pardon me for not wanting to sing day and night! Being cooped up in this cage doesn't exactly create the proper mood!" said Cornelius, swallowing another berry.

"Just try. Strike a pose. Sing. He'll love it."

"Like this? You can't be serious!" Cornelius perched on the dogwood branch and preened his primary and secondary feathers, adjusting them perfectly, and lifted his head as though to sing.

"That's perfect. Promise me!"

"All right, all right! I promise!"

The nearby snoring stopped, and Joseph sat up. He scratched his head as he shuffled over to his desk, then let out a gasp.

"Little One!" he cried. "You came home! Where have you been?"

He gathered up Celeste and cradled her next to his cheek, stroking her and giving her tiny kisses on her ears. "I have missed you so much! You're a brave little critter to come home to me!"

Celeste burrowed between his palms and wriggled rapturously, relishing the warmth and safety of his gentle hands. Joseph found a few peanuts for her, then slipped her into her usual spot in his shirt pocket.

Smiling, he then peered into the little wooden cage. "Good mornin' to you, my friend!" he said to Cornelius. "Here's a little present!" From a dish on his desk he retrieved several ripe but somewhat squished blackberries. "Here you go. Eat up!"

Cornelius eyed the berries.

"Come, my friend, you have to eat and keep up your strength. We're counting on you for a fine painting, you know. If only I could get the background right . . . Hey! I see Mr. Audubon added a branch to your little home. This would make a good background for the painting." Joseph went to the desk and gathered up some pencils.

Celeste squeaked from the shirt pocket, "*Psst!* Cornelius! Now's the time!"

Cornelius hopped gracefully onto the dogwood branch, fluttering a bit. He took a deep breath and opened his mouth to sing.

Out came the liquid, gurgling stream of silvery notes so sweet and fluid that Joseph dropped his pencils.

"My Lord . . . such music!" Joseph whispered just as Cornelius sang again. The song, a mixture of sweetness and melancholy, swirled through the room like a cool breeze.

Joseph immediately took up drawing materials again and then sat in a chair in front of the cage. This time as he worked there was no eraser needed; graceful lines of dogwood leaves flowed from his eyes and down into his hand, then out onto the paper. As Joseph worked, Cornelius lifted his head to sing again. Joseph smiled and attacked his work with even greater enthusiasm.

The paint box came out next. Soon the page was covered with the soft greens of the leaves and bright reds of the dogwood berries.

There was a knock at the door, and Audubon stepped into the room.

"Working so early, Joseph?" he asked.

"Yes, *monsieur*," he replied. "The morning light and . . . everything . . . was just right."

Audubon stood in front of the thrush painting. His brows arched up.

"Ah . . . Joseph. I see my instruction has inspired you. This is beautiful. Your dogwood is perfect."

Joseph stepped back from his work. It *was* perfect. The wood thrush in the painting was now at home among the leaves and twigs of the dogwood tree, and Joseph could see that it was just right.

He smiled at the wood thrush. "Thank you, Mr. Thrush!" he whispered.

Celeste smiled. Her plan had worked.

CHAPTER TWENTY-FIVE
Cornelius Says Adieu

The crickets and cicadas were beginning their chorus. Supper was being served downstairs in the dining room.

Celeste balanced her way up the dogwood branch, using it like a ladder to reach the cage door latch. The branch was just tall enough. "Hey!" she squeaked in delight. "The wire is gone! What happened?"

The twisted wire that had held the cage door closed had been replaced by a small length of rope, looped and knotted several times around the twigs.

"Good news! The wire snapped when the boy was opening the cage yesterday, so he latched the door with a piece of rope." Cornelius explained. "Isn't that better? Can you untie it, or nibble through it?"

"You bet I can!" It took a while, but Celeste bit and yanked, chewed and gnawed until finally the cage door swung open.

"Freedom!" Cornelius trilled. In a flash he was through the cage door and circling the room.

Celeste leaped over to the drawing desk, and

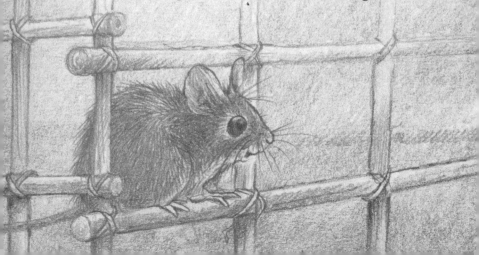

Cornelius settled near her on the windowsill.

They looked at the watercolor painting on the desk: a wood thrush was stretching up to eat a dogwood berry. The painting was soft, with cinnamon browns and forest greens.

"It looks just like me," marveled Cornelius.

"It does, indeed. Now you'll live forever in a painting."

"Maybe he'll paint you next. . . . When I come back, you can show me your portrait!"

"Come back? Come back from where? Where are you going?"

Cornelius looked earnestly at his friend. "I'm going away, flying south. I go away this time every year. I'm leaving very soon; in fact, that's why it's so perfect that I'm out of that cage now."

Celeste felt panicky. "But why? Why do you have to go?"

"We all go," Cornelius replied. "All the wood

thrushes. We go to where it's summertime all year round."

A group of thrushes suddenly flew into the magnolia outside, spilling among the branches and chattering. Celeste and Cornelius looked at each other.

"Well, I guess this is farewell, for now," Cornelius said.

Celeste hadn't counted on this. She was nearly overwhelmed with a heaviness of heart; she was going to miss her friend. Her eyes began to burn, and a tiny tear spilled out.

"Yes, I guess so," she replied. Her throat tightened, and her ears folded back. "When will you be back?"

"In the spring." But Cornelius seemed distracted and slightly agitated. There was something powerful inside him, a compass in his brain, telling him: *Fly south*.

Celeste scrambled up the drapes to the sill. She looked at the thrush for a moment and held out her paw to stroke the soft feathers of his cheek.

Cornelius stretched one wing, then the other. His eyes were bright. He spread his tail feathers, testing them. He was ready to go. He needed to go; instinct was telling him so.

"Good-bye," he said softly. "And thank you. You're a good friend."

His wings opened; and he dropped from the sill, arching dizzily in the air below the window, then out and beyond the garden hedges, gathering with the other thrushes. The flock of them circled around, and Cornelius looked back to glance once more at Celeste. He called out, "Good-bye! Good-bye! See you in the spring!" and off he flew, flapping and looking very happy, almost giddy.

Celeste watched the flock of thrushes get smaller and smaller. She tried to follow Cornelius with her eyes, but the birds crisscrossed and wove among one another in the air, and soon she couldn't tell which of the tiny, disappearing dots was her friend.

Was this a part of friendship, too? The hardship of saying good-bye? Suddenly her eyes blurred . . . but just as suddenly her skin felt prickly. Her whiskers twitched.

She wasn't alone.

She looked down.

Something had heard her cries. There was the cat, eyes black and focused, hind legs poised and ready to lunge.

CHAPTER TWENTY-SIX
The Attic

Celeste skittered across the desk, trying to hide in the folds of the drapes just as the cat leaped up. With her heart in her throat, she lightly flew down through the creases of the brocade and then raced along the wall, frantically trying to find a place of safety.

The cat saw the curtains move, quickly followed the movement down, and jumped back to the floor. It would not let the mouse escape again.

Celeste headed straight to the bedroom door and out into the hallway. She looked for an escape. In a flash she saw there was only one option: Straight ahead was a small knothole at the bottom of a door. The hole looked just large enough, she thought, to squeeze through. Of course, she had no idea what was on the other side of the door, but what fate could be worse than the needle-sharp teeth and merciless claws of the cat?

She raced to the door, the cat inches behind her. She felt her tail slip between the cat's claws as, with a frantic wiggle, she made it through the knothole. The cat's head slammed into the door just behind her. Immediately, a paw was thrust through the knothole, with hooked claws extended.

Celeste looked up, gasping, breathless. A set of steps loomed in front of her.

"More stairs? Higher still?" Her mind raced as she glanced behind her. The cat's claws were still making vicious swipes through the knothole. "Well, no cat can get through this hole, at least." She caught her breath and headed up the stairs.

Celeste climbed the steps, one by one, until at last all fourteen stairs were scaled. She was out of breath and fatigued as she had never been before, almost too tired to care where she was.

Celeste reached the top step. She surveyed her whereabouts.

Lemony yellow sunlight filtered through dust motes from several windows. A high, beamed ceiling angled above her head.

Hills and valleys of unimagined treasures spread in all directions. To her right, Celeste noticed a vast field of old feather tick mattresses. They were piled in a slanted heap against a weathered-looking table, on top of which sat a cracked oil lamp.

To the left was a mountain of trunks and chests covered with dusty sheets speckled with bird droppings. Straight ahead, Celeste saw a stack of old books tied into a bundle with twine, a broken spinning wheel, a chair with a sagging cane seat, a stack of old dishes, a tangle of woolens hanging moth eaten on a line. There were old crates and trunks and satchels and chests.

Celeste was exhausted. It had been a long, arduous several days. The field of striped ticking looked inviting, and easy to climb. She scaled the mountain of feather mattresses. There was a small rip in the side of one; she crawled in, curled up in the feathers, and fell asleep.

CHAPTER TWENTY-SEVEN

A Friend Returns

She slept for a long time. Life on the plantation continued its pattern: The mules pulled the rattling wagons to the fields and back, the chickens and geese pecked at bugs around the smokehouse. Meals were cooked, chores were begun and completed. Garden spiders wove webs in the crape myrtles. Bees visited the okra and squash blossoms. Viridian hoverflies darted among the rosemary and lavender and lemon balm in the herb garden. The live oaks sent long shadows toward the west, then to the east.

Celeste finally awoke to the sound of shouting voices coming from downstairs. One of them she knew was Joseph's voice, and she scampered down the attic steps, pausing at the knothole; she feared the cat might be lurking nearby. Light from an oil lamp glowed beneath Joseph's bedroom doorway. Loud voices mixed with a shrieking, screeching call and the sounds of flapping feathers.

"Tie him, quickly!" shouted a deep voice. She recognized it as Audubon's. "And tightly! Here!"

After more scuffling sounds the room quieted. Celeste started across the hallway, then hesitated.

"Ah, yes. He's a beauty!" said Audubon. "Mr. Pirrie isn't a bad shot after all!"

Then she heard Joseph. "And he'll heal up fine. He'll be a great live model for the osprey painting."

Osprey! Celeste thought in alarm.

Audubon paused. "Yes," he said. "There is something about this one. . . . He has spirit."

Suddenly the bedroom door swung open, and Audubon and Joseph entered the dim hallway. "Once you've gotten the supplies we need in New Orleans, return straight back, Joseph," Audubon was saying. "If you leave tonight, you can be back by Saturday."

"Yes, sir."

Leaving? thought Celeste. *Going away?* She felt panicky inside.

Joseph glanced back into the room, searching for something.

"Where did she wander off to?" he asked.

Audubon arched an eyebrow. "Who?"

"My little helper. Little One. She's disappeared. I put out some nuts for her, but she's gone."

"Perhaps the cat got her."

"No, she's much too keen for that to have happened. But I feel a little lost without her, without her in my pocket. She's my companion, my . . . friend."

"Well, I'll keep an eye out for the little mouse; you

get on your way to New Orleans."

Celeste pressed against the wall, avoiding the heavy shoes as Audubon and Joseph strode down the hall. She wanted to squeal and squeak and run after Joseph; but she hesitated, fearing the giant Dash, who trotted at their heels. They turned the corner, then clomped down the stairs, their voices dimming as they headed out the front door.

Again Celeste heard flapping sounds from the bedroom, then the crash of an object falling and pieces of something scattering on the floor. The flapping stopped.

She peeked around the door.

There, tied to the footboard of the bed, was a large brown-and-white bird. It turned its sunflower yellow eyes toward Celeste.

A familiar voice squawked, "It's impolite to stare, you know!"

"Lafayette! What happened? What are you doing here?" Celeste raced across the floor and up to the bed rail, and gave the osprey a hug around his leg.

Lafayette grinned. "I'm glad to see you, too, dumplin'."

"But I heard such a commotion! I had no idea it would be you!"

"You'd make a commotion, too, honey pie, if you were tied up. And look at this." He gestured to a putrefying catfish head nearby. "They expect me to eat that? That fish has been dead longer than my Great-aunt Mabel, and I'm getting just a little bit tired of the stink!"

Celeste sniffed in agreement.

"You're wonderin' how I got myself here, am I right, lamb chop?"

"Oh, yes!"

"Well, there I was, mindin' my own business after droppin' you on the windowsill, had barely gotten any distance at all, and the next thing I know, *BOOM!* Some crazy maniac down in the yard is jumpin' around and wavin' his gun and laughin'! My wing is missin' some feathers, and down I go. I got a good jab at somebody's hand, though. . . . You should have seen the blood! Now I'm tied up here . . . tied up because my good wing is strong enough to get me up in the air. . . . I'd try to take off right now if it weren't for these straps."

"What are they going to do with you?"

"Over there on the table are his sketches. He spends hours studyin' me and scribblin' on sheets of paper. Then he gets all flustered and stomps off. Meanwhile,

here I sit with Mr. Stinky B. Catfish, and I'm about to go crazy!"

Celeste noticed the thick leather strap that tied Lafayette to the footboard.

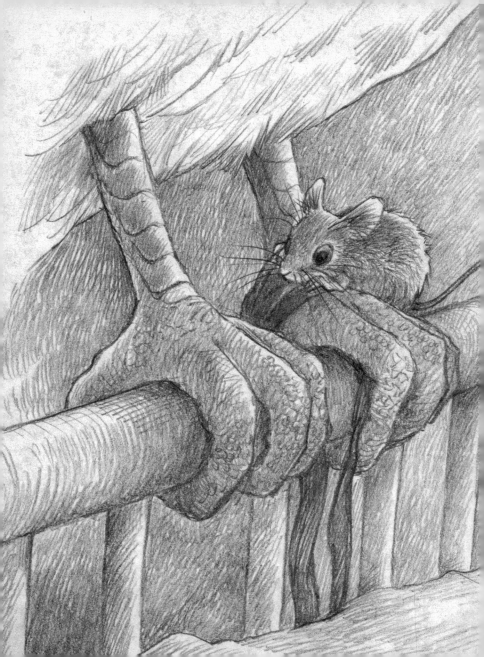

"Perhaps I could chew through those," she said. "The window's open. You could just fly out."

"You could do that?"

"Of course!"

"Excellent idea!" Lafayette exclaimed. "Start chewin', sugar pie!"

Celeste scrambled over and, sitting on Lafayette's left foot, began to gnaw. It was difficult; the leather strap was hard and tough. In half an hour she was only partway through the strap.

Just then they heard the slam of the

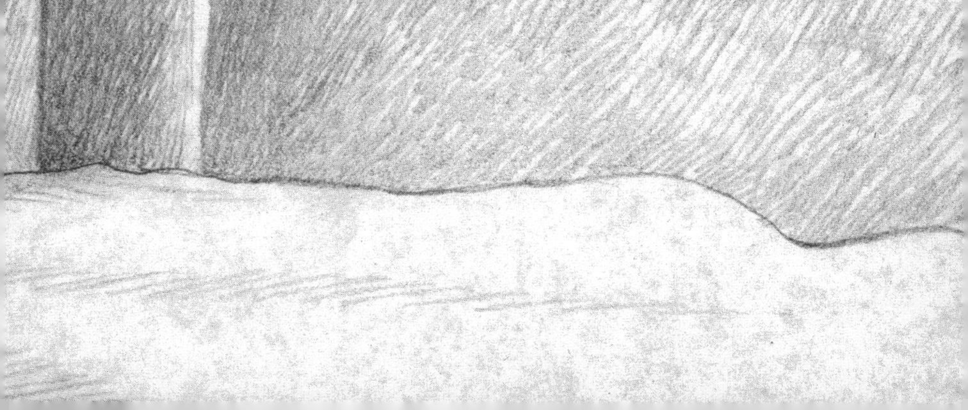

screen door downstairs and the heavy sound of boots coming up the stairs.

"He's back." The osprey sighed. "The bigger one. I can tell by the footsteps."

Celeste darted across the bed and leaped over to a nightstand, hiding behind the washbasin.

The tall, imposing figure of Audubon appeared in the doorway. He stood with hands on hips, the thick shank of auburn hair hanging to his shoulders, studying Lafayette in the lamplight.

Lafayette glowered back, sitting hunched and tense. He had had enough of this man who sat watching him for hours and hours, scratching lines on paper.

"We begin again," Audubon said, grabbing his supplies and sitting on a stool in front of the osprey.

From her hiding place Celeste could see over Audubon's shoulder. His eyes were fixed on Lafayette. Pencil line after pencil line covered the large piece of paper. Over and over the lines were erased, then begun again.

The room was hot; Audubon's face glistened with perspiration.

Lafayette's anger slowly gave way to boredom. He sat on the bed rail half asleep.

Celeste watched Audubon's hand, fascinated. The way it glided and flowed across the paper reminded her of her own paw as it moved in rhythm when she was weaving.

Suddenly it stopped. The pencil fell to the floor as Audubon dropped his face into his hands and sighed with exasperation, shoulders slumped.

"Mon Dieu," he moaned. "My drawing is all wrong." He stood up, sheets of paper spilling off his lap. He paced the room several times, thinking, his chin in his hand.

"Perhaps," he said, contemplating Lafayette yet again, "I need to pin your wings up, holding them in place . . . and then your head needs to be wired upright. . . . I could make a better painting. . . ."

Celeste nearly squeaked in alarm, peeking out from behind the washbasin.

But Audubon picked up his pencils; again there was the sound of graphite scratching on paper, then he suddenly stamped his foot.

"Ça n'est pas possible!" his voice erupted. "There is no *life* in this portrait! This osprey might as well be dead and stuffed like a Christmas goose! The wings are folded like it is in a casket! And the eyes . . . dull! The neck . . . stiff! The feet . . . how you say it? Crooked! I cannot get it correct. My paintings are as blank and lifeless as the portraits of Monsieur and Madame Pirrie in the dining room downstairs!"

There was a clatter of pencils being thrown across the room as Audubon stormed out. The large piece of paper drifted to the floor, sliding nearly to the door.

Celeste ducked a little closer into the shadows, but she could see the lines of a large bird drawn on the paper.

Celeste studied the drawing. She had a plan. It had worked before, and it would work again.

CHAPTER TWENTY-EIGHT
Lafayette Strikes a Pose

Celeste once again climbed up to the bed rail and began gnawing at the leather tie. She stopped for a moment.

"Look," she said. "I've got an idea. You're going to think it's a bit odd, but please trust me."

"Okeydokey, sugar plum, I trust you. What's the idea?"

"When Monsieur Audubon returns, he's going to sketch you again, correct?"

"Correct."

"And he's going to try over and over, and get very frustrated, correct?"

"Correct."

"And he's going to try and capture your beauty with pencil and paper, correct?"

"Correct."

"And if he doesn't get it right, you may end up stuffed and pinned, correct?"

"I prefer not to think about that, if you don't mind, peach blossom."

Celeste giggled. "Well, so, you need to help him!"

"Come again?"

"Pose! Be yourself, but pose. Help him out."

"Help him out? He's got me tied up here like a prisoner, and you want me to help him out?"

"Would you do it, for me?"

"Well, what'll I do, darlin'?" queried the osprey. "Jump up and down? Clamor around like a parakeet? I'm new at this, you know."

"Pretend that you're on top of the tallest sycamore tree you can think of," said Celeste, hardly daring to whisper. "Like you're just about to scream out across the river. Wings up! Look excited! Look dangerous! Look . . . *alive!*"

Lafayette pondered for a moment, then he raised his wings and opened his beak as if to call out.

"The back wing up, the wing in front down a bit," directed Celeste.

"You've got to be pulling my leg! Why in the world would I do this?"

"Hold it right there!" whispered Celeste. "That's

it! Don't move a feather!"

The osprey froze in place. "Like this? You sure? I feel ridiculous!"

"You look great! This is going to be perfect!"

"He's going to think I'm about to attack!"

As if on cue, the heavy tread of Mr. Audubon's boots could be heard climbing the stairs, then walking down the hallway.

"*Shh!* He's coming back! Don't move!" squeaked

Celeste as she scampered to a hiding place.

The boots turned into the studio doorway.

"Mon Dieu!" Audubon gasped, staring at the osprey. *"C'est ça! Parfait! Toi! Le beau spécimen!* You are magnificent!" He stared for nearly a minute, then grabbed a large piece of watercolor paper and a handful of pencils and began to sketch.

There, in front of her, Celeste watched as Lafayette's body and wings began to form on the paper. Only an outline at first, but feathers, streaks, spots, and other details soon followed. Audubon's pencil raced in every direction; his eyes, bright with excitement, studied the bird's every feather.

He drew a gaping beak, opened as though screaming across a valley, and wings outstretched in flight. "I'll put a fish in your talons, like you have just pulled it from the Mississippi," he said out loud.

Next, out came a wooden box of watercolors.

Celeste couldn't help herself as she crawled out from behind the paint box. Mesmerized, she watched Audubon use a variety of soft brushes and an old shaving mug filled with water as he transformed the penciled outline into an osprey full of chocolate brown and tawny cream. A golden yellow eye blazed fiercely. He added a background sky of cool blues.

At last the artist sat back. He stretched his long arms and smiled at the osprey.

"*Merci*, my friend," he said; and he lay on the bed, asleep within several ticks of a clock.

Lafayette blinked and lowered his wings. He glanced over at the paint box lid. Celeste smiled approvingly.

CHAPTER TWENTY-NINE
Freedom

A h! You're almost there, Celeste!" whispered Lafayette encouragingly. "Just a little bit more."

Celeste felt her jaw muscles ache. Gnawing tough leather was not easy.

"A little more . . . just a little more . . . Yes! That's it!"

The heavy leather strap fell to the floor, and Lafayette leaped up with a flap of wings.

They glanced at the bed; Audubon was snoring peacefully.

"Pumpkin pie," Lafayette said, "you are one good friend to have around! My, oh my, but does this feel

good. Thank you, darlin', from the bottom of my ever-lovin' heart!"

"You're welcome," she said, rubbing her swollen jaw.

"If I can ever be of any service, don't hesitate to give a shout, anytime, day or night. I am forever obliged." Lafayette gave a little bow.

"Would you come visit me?" queried Celeste.

"Well, sugar lamb, I'll definitely be keeping an eye on you," promised the osprey. He nodded at his wing. "But it may be a while before I come for a visit. It's a dangerous world out there. Now, you be careful, you hear?"

"You be careful, too, Lafayette." Celeste smiled.

And with that the osprey flapped to the open window, tested his lame wing, leaped joyfully into the air, and was gone.

CHAPTER THIRTY
A Discovery

Celeste decided that, until Joseph returned, the safest place to be was in the attic, where the knothole entrance kept out the menacing inhabitants of the house. The nest she made in the old feather mattress was cozy, safe, and quiet.

She decided to explore her attic home a bit

more. Scaling to the summit of the mountain of mattresses, she studied her new domain. Across the way next to the window, which was missing a pane, she saw another mountain: a draped sheet.

Celeste crawled under the old sheet and blinked. In the musty shadows she saw—or did she see? —a tiny, mouse-sized chair. And was that a miniature tasseled pillow? Amid a confused jumble of chair legs and patterned fabrics Celeste could discern what looked

to be a complete and perfect dining room . . . made for a mouse!

There were tiny, ornate picture frames, carved and beveled, holding tiny pictures: a still life, a portrait, a country landscape. Clustered around a tiny dining table were several chairs, each with a needlepoint seat.

Celeste made her way past a corner cabinet with glass doors; she puffed on a pane and wiped it gingerly with her paw. Inside she saw plates and cups and saucers, pieces from a blue-and-white china set. Opening a cabinet door below, she found what looked to be a tablecloth.

She passed through a doorway and entered another room. The light was a little better here, and she noted the lavender-striped wallpaper.

"This must be the living room," she whispered. A beautiful sofa, just her size, covered in maroon velvet, lay on its back. Two chairs and several small tables were also overturned. A fireplace and mantel had been artfully painted on one wall. Over it was the oval portrait of a young girl; her face looked familiar. A set of stairs in one corner of the living room led to another story above.

Celeste climbed the stairs and then tiptoed her way into a bedroom. As with the rooms below, the contents here were also tossed about and covered in dust: a small bed and nightstand, an oval hooked rug, and a ladder-back chair painted orange. A washbasin and pitcher lay on the floor. Next to the bed was another door.

Celeste passed reverently into the last room.

Through the dim light she saw an enormous four-poster bed covered with a soft, pink blanket. Two satin pillows were trimmed in tiny lace ribbon. Beside the bed was a small table draped with a lace cloth. Against one wall stood a wooden armoire with flowers and vines painted up the sides and on each door. A large, overstuffed chair sat perched on a small rug. The walls were covered in flowery wallpaper, making

Celeste feel as though she were in a magical garden.

"This is the most beautiful room that has ever been," she murmured to herself.

The bed looked comfy and inviting; Celeste ran her hand along the soft blanket and then crawled up. The bed was stuffed with cotton bolls, and she sank blissfully into it, head plopped onto a silk pillow.

"I've found *home*," she said to herself. "There is nowhere else I'd rather be." She smiled and fell asleep.

And indeed, it was a lovely nest for a mouse.

CHAPTER THIRTY-ONE
Housecleaning

The draped sheet over Celeste's new home made it feel close and dim, dusty and airless. She scampered to the floor and pondered.

Gathering a corner of the sheet in her mouth, she bit tightly. With claws gripping the rough oak floorboards, she leaned forward and pulled fiercely. Slowly the dusty sheet moved with her, inch by inch. Finally, in a rush of fragile and yellowing cotton, it slipped into a pile in front of the dollhouse, producing a haze of dust.

Celeste began straightaway to clean and make order of her new home. Now that the house was bright and cheery, and its contents easy to see, she could open drawers, explore cabinets, shake out linens, polish brass, shine crockery, and sweep floors.

And that she did. She made a small broom using feathers from the old mattresses and a rag from a bit of mattress ticking. Soon the floors and walnut staircase glowed. She dusted and polished the chandelier and glass cabinet doors.

An inventory of the dining-room cabinet revealed a lace tablecloth, four china plates with matching cups and saucers, and a china serving platter. In one drawer Celeste found several tiny candles, partially melted from the summer heat in the attic.

She pulled one of the chairs from the living room out onto the windowsill. The missing pane afforded her the chance of catching a passing breeze, and from her perch she could see the comings and goings of the plantation below.

Celeste felt contented after days of hard work. She straightened one last picture, fluffed up a sofa cushion, and then at last made her way to her bedroom.

Beams of a peach-colored sunset washed across the wallpaper, and the tiny room glowed with coppery peonies and amber hyacinths. A breeze, fragrant with ripening grapes from the garden arbor, drifted through the missing windowpane.

Celeste could now see out the window from her perch on the bed. Over and beyond the treetops lay an expanse of sunset-drenched lawn and fields and forest. Even the dusty windowpanes couldn't dull the brilliant scene as Celeste lay on her soft, cottony bed. She nibbled on a watermelon seed, staring in rapture at the landscape stretching so far. A mockingbird was singing in the nearby magnolia.

She missed Joseph. She wished Cornelius or Lafayette were there.

At that moment there were two feelings inside Celeste's tiny, rapidly beating heart that made her feel as full, and as empty, as a gourd. The sheer beauty of this moment was perfect and sublime. But she was alone.

The golden edges of the clouds faded to soft pinks, then to gray blues; and finally the sky darkened. A few stars appeared. Celeste crawled under the soft blanket, tucking her nose under her paw, and sank into sleep.

CHAPTER THIRTY-TWO

A Homecoming of Sorts

When she awoke, Celeste realized that laboring over her chores had worked up an appetite. She gathered two baskets and headed down the attic stairs and through the knothole.

The hallway was dark. Celeste scampered past Joseph's room, then quickly stopped. Her ears flicked, her whiskers quivered, and her heart felt a sudden fullness. Was that the sound of his pencil sketching? She felt dispirited when she realized it was just the distant ticking of the hallway clock downstairs.

The dining room seemed unusually still. There were leftover crumbs and bits dotted across the carpet, but certainly no bounty. The dining-room carpet had been swept. She sniffed the air for traces of cat.

Ducking beneath the sideboard for a short rest, she let out a tiny cry of surprise. The hole was no longer there: A short wooden board had been nailed to the wall, sealing off the entrance, and the emergency escape route, forever.

She evenly distributed her meager spoils between the two baskets, securing the straps across her shoulders. She studied the dining room and then ran cautiously toward the stairs.

The looming clock suddenly struck five, startling Celeste so that she left tiny claw marks in the waxy patina of the oak floorboard. Her heart beat furiously.

Some inner feeling was nagging at her. She sniffed the air again and again. Her whiskers twitched nonstop.

The journey across the hall, up the newel post and the stair rail seemed routine now, although still arduous. But there was a faint feline odor hanging in the air. Her dark eyes pierced the dim hallway, but there was no other sign of the cat.

Celeste reached the end of the upstairs hallway, then stopped in her tracks. The scent of cat fur and cat paws and cat breath quickly thickened, like a soupy mist moving in off the river. She saw it now: the dark, cloudy shape of the cat crouched and waiting, staring motionlessly at the knothole in the attic door, between Celeste and home. The cat didn't see or hear Celeste. It seemed completely fascinated by the hole in the door.

Celeste hid as best as she could in the shadow of a bookcase that stood against the wall. She waited.

Rescue came in the unlikely form of Eliza Pirrie.

There was a swishing sound from the hallway downstairs and then continuing up the steps. Celeste pressed her body against the bookcase as Eliza glided by, inches away.

"There you are, Puss!" she exclaimed, hurrying to gather up the gray cat, who glared at her from the base of the attic door. "You've been hiding from me! Shame on you, Puss! Time for your breakfast!" Eliza carried the cat down the stairs, fussing and cooing. Celeste made a dash for the attic knothole.

It was a relief to be within the relative safety of the attic, and Celeste smiled contentedly at the thought of her warm, cottony bed with the soft satin pillows.

She unpacked her goodies, stowed her baskets, and nibbled a bread crumb as she made her way up the steps to her bedroom.

"Well, well, well," squeaked a vaguely familiar voice. "You finally made it home. I hope you brought back something to eat."

Celeste stared as the cool, gray, dawn light came creeping into the bedroom. There, stretched across her bed, pinched face and beady eyes poking out from beneath the pink blanket, was Trixie.

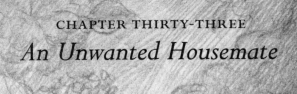

CHAPTER THIRTY-THREE

An Unwanted Housemate

Cat got your tongue, Celeste?" Trixie yawned, showing her pointy teeth and fleshy gums. "What do you have there . . . a bread crumb? I'd have thought you'd bring

home something more substantial than that. There better be more downstairs."

Celeste felt all her blood surge to her feet; they seemed frozen to the floor. Her ears buzzed, and her mouth was dry. She stifled a gurgled cry, as suddenly her nest seemed unsafe, uncertain, and unhappy.

"Yes, it's me," continued Trixie. "Don't look so surprised. Aren't you happy to see me?"

"Trixie! Yes . . . yes, of course!" Celeste felt her voice stumble. "It's just so unexpected!"

"I hid in the cellar for weeks. I saw you one night from the dining room as you were heading up the stairs. I wondered why you were going up and so I followed you. That darned cat almost got me this morning. Well . . . don't just stand there like a ninny; go fetch me something to eat. I found your stash of raisins, and the piece of pork rind."

"You ate the pork rind? All of it?" Celeste had been saving it for several dinners that week.

"Yes, all of it! That snively little morsel was barely a mouthful. And what's that thing?" Trixie pointed to the nearby gondola on the windowsill. "Still making these silly baskets, I see. It looks like you got a little carried away with this one."

"Yes, you could say that," replied Celeste.

"How do you carry food in this? It'd be too heavy once it was filled."

"It wasn't made for food, Trixie. It was made for me."

"Come again?"

"I took a ride in it. A friend, an osprey, carried the basket with me in it and took me for a ride."

"What?"

"My friend Lafayette carried the basket, and we went all over the countryside. It was wonderful."

"You're lying. That's impossible."

Celeste was quiet.

Trixie glared at her. "If this osprey—whatever that

is—who took you on a trip around the countryside is such a good friend, then he wouldn't mind taking *me* on one, too, would he?"

"Oh, I couldn't ask Lafaye—"

"Why not? You think you're so, so special, don't you? So high and mighty, living in this fancy place, going on flying trips. . . . You're just too good for your old friends now, is that it?"

"No, Trixie, it's just that I couldn't ask . . ."

"Look, you tell your friend that Miss Trixie wants to be taken for a ride. Tell him that I want to go *higher*, and *farther*, than *you*! Tell him that!"

"Well, you see, Trixie . . ."

"Tell him!"

CHAPTER THIRTY-FOUR

Trixie Takes Off . . .

Celeste watched for Lafayette above the treetops, returning from a fishing trip; and after a few days she spotted his flapping and gliding silhouette. She waved and raced back and forth across the sill, signaling to him.

Lafayette was surprised to meet Trixie. He didn't understand why Celeste seemed different, too. She was very quiet and wouldn't look him in the eye. But he agreed to take Trixie for a ride in the gondola, and Trixie clambered in.

"You made this thing too small!" she complained.

Celeste and Lafayette exchanged looks. Trixie was a tight fit after days of eating Celeste's food and endlessly snoozing on the settee. The blades of dried grass strained against her girth as Trixie squeezed in as much of herself as she could.

"Well, what next?" she shrieked nervously. "I haven't got all day." Her eyes widened as she glanced down at the ground perilously far below. She dug her claws tightly into the rim of the basket.

With powerful flaps Lafayette lifted into the air, then grasped hold of the gondola handles. It dragged for a moment on the windowsill and then lurched into the sky.

"Hey! Mind yourself! Precious cargo down here, you know!" Trixie cried out.

With a swoop and a series of flaps, Lafayette and his passenger disappeared behind the treetops.

Celeste watched them go and then set about having

a blissfully peaceful morning, relishing the time she had in her home without Trixie's braying voice invading her thoughts. She tiptoed through the house, savoring every single second of solitude, touching the furniture, sliding her paw along the flowers of the wallpaper, listening to nothing but the birds and insects in the garden outside. *That's it*, Celeste thought. *I've lost my home yet again. Trixie has stolen it from me.*

She sat in her chair on the windowsill and watched the sky beyond the trees for Trixie's return. "Lafayette sure is taking her on a long ride," she said to herself, scanning the horizon.

CHAPTER THIRTY-FIVE

. . . *Like a Rock Tossed Into a Muddy Pond*

Meanwhile, Lafayette struggled with his passenger. Trixie was absorbed in screaming directions and was completely oblivious to the beauty of the awakening landscape.

"You're going too fast!" Trixie screamed up to him. "You're going too high! And don't flap so hard. . . . Feathers make me sneeze, you know!"

They approached the river. A thick, silvery, early-morning mist blanketed it.

"Where's the river?" hollered Trixie. She shifted and twisted in the basket, squirming in an attempt at being comfortable in the tiny space.

"It's right below us!" Lafayette called back. "We're almost exactly over the middle of the river, ma'am. This is the widest point for miles. Sorry about the mist; makes it kind of hard to see much; but it's mighty pretty anyway, don't you think?"

The morning sun was catching the tips of the clouds, making the higher puffs pink and gold and orange.

"I don't see what all the excitement is about," replied Trixie. "This basket is too cramped. And I'm feeling a little queasy. This flying business is for the birds!"

"Want me to turn around?"

"Yes, I want you to turn around! Take me home. I need to lie down. Celeste better have breakfast ready when I get there."

"Poor Celeste . . ." Lafayette mumbled.

"What did you say?"

"Oh, nothing, ma'am. I'm just gonna turn to head back." And with that Lafayette gently banked his wings, and the pair headed toward the rising sun.

"Hurry up!" Trixie yelled. "It's getting past my breakfast time." To emphasize her point she yanked

sharply on the gondola strap.

"But, ma'am, don't you want to ride up along the river a bit? The fog will rise soon, and you'll have quite a view."

"I said, Hurry up! I'm hungry! The only view I want is of a plate full of food!"

With that she gave the strap another hard yank. In an instant, one end snapped, and the basket almost fell away completely. Trixie scrambled and clawed but could not grasp the strap soon enough. She plummeted down, grabbing at air, disappearing into the river mist like a rock tossed into a muddy pond.

Lafayette felt himself lift and bob upward, surprised by the sudden drop in weight.

"What the . . . Miss Trixie?" he called out as he looked down and saw only the dangling basket.

"Miss Trixie! Oh, holy crawdad! Miss Trixie!" he called again and again, circling and fanning out

above the mist. He swooped down, gliding just over the surface of the water, but heard no cries, saw no splashing.

Trixie was gone.

It seemed like hours before Celeste at last saw Lafayette's silhouette against the midmorning sun. She squinted; it looked as if the osprey was flying very fast, faster than she had seen him fly before. And the basket: It was dangling and fluttering below Lafayette . . . and it was empty.

Celeste raced back and forth across the sill. "What happened? Where's Trixie?"

"Darlin', it just happened. Weren't nobody's fault, 'cept maybe Miss Trixie's for eatin' more than she ought'n to have. But she pulled on the basket handle, and one end broke, and down she went, right smack dab into the river. I went lookin' for her, up and down the river, lookin' at where the currents might

have taken her; but . . . I'm terribly sorry, sweetheart, about your loss; but that's how it happened.
I'm afraid Miss Trixie won't be comin' back."

CHAPTER THIRTY-SIX

Back from New Orleans

Trixie didn't return, but Joseph did—back from New Orleans. From her windowsill Celeste heard the shouts of greeting as a horse trotted up the lane, and her pulse quickened as she saw Joseph was the rider. "He's back!" she squeaked, scampering down the attic steps. Joseph yelped in delight when he found her perched on his worktable.

"Little One! You're back! I knew you'd come back. I hoped and I prayed . . . but I knew you would." Joseph produced a walnut meat; and Celeste wiggled and squirmed deliriously, happy to be back in Joseph's shirt pocket.

"You should have seen the city, Little One," he said. "So much to see. All sorts of shops and markets, and so many people. The streets full of rich folks, poor folks, all kinds. I saw some fancy buggies, and beautiful horses. And at night the streets all lit up with gas lamps. And the smells! You need to be mighty careful where you step, let me tell you. I don't know how they stand it—the smells—day after day. But New Orleans is quite a place."

He gently fished Celeste out from his pocket and nuzzled her to his chin. "I missed you, Little One. I had no one to talk to. I'd find myself talking like you were there. I'd say, 'Look at that cage of nonpareils, Little One,' or 'Have you ever laid eyes on a lady with hair the color of a melon before, Little One?'"

They heard the big farm bell ringing outside; it was suppertime.

"I know better than to take you with me. Now, you be a good little mouse and stay here while I go eat some vittles." Grabbing his bandanna, he fashioned her a nest and left her there on the desk. "I'll be back."

Celeste began to think of her attic home. "One short trip up the stairs," she said to herself. "Just to see it one more time. I'll be back before supper is over."

Across the hallway she darted to the attic steps. She slipped through the knothole just as the cat was

sauntering its way down the hallway toward her.

Keenly aware of the fresh scent of mouse, the cat positioned itself at the knothole.

Celeste heard the clock downstairs chime one, two, three, all hours until the sun was nearly up. Finally, at dawn, Joseph returned from supper, calling for her, searching the room not far away. But he was exhausted after his journey from New Orleans and soon collapsed on the cot in a dead sleep. Still the cat sat and patiently watched the knothole.

Finally, near dawn, Celeste climbed the attic steps and nestled in her bed. She closed her eyes, thinking, *I'll help Joseph with his paintings later. He'll feed me nuts and scratch under my chin. That cat can't guard the attic door forever.*

CHAPTER THIRTY-SEVEN
Departure

The summer was ending. Cicadas droned lazily in the surrounding treetops. The mockingbird, after a hiatus during the heat of dog days, was singing again from inside the magnolia. A golden haze spread across the sky to the west.

Celeste woke from a long, deep sleep to the sound of a horse whinnying. She looked out her window.

Down below, three horses stood in the shade of a pecan tree. Men were loading supplies and belongings onto one of the horses; Celeste recognized Audubon and Mr. Pirrie among them. She saw the dark shape of the gray cat sitting idly among the roots of the pecan tree, looking bored. *At least now I can safely head back to Joseph's room,* she thought.

As the men worked, Celeste noticed that more than the usual amount of supplies and goods were being loaded—too many things were being strapped to the back of the packhorse, including large, flat bundles carefully wrapped. "Those are the paintings," Celeste whispered to herself.

Then her heartbeat quickened as she saw Joseph coming from inside the house, carrying a saddlebag. She could hear the men talking.

"That everything, Joseph?" Audubon asked.

"Yes, sir. Well, almost everything."

"Almost?"

"Yes, sir. I can't find Little . . . I can't find my mouse." He eyed the gray cat under the magnolia. "I can't just leave her here."

Audubon frowned at Joseph. "It's a mouse. Tighten those satchel straps. We're ready to go. Monsieur Pirrie, we bid you *adieu*."

In a heartbeat Celeste realized what was happening; Joseph was leaving, and he wasn't coming back.

The supplies he brought back from New Orleans were in preparation for a journey away from here.

She felt panicky. She leaped from the sill, her feet flying as fast as a honeybee's wings down the attic steps, out through the knothole, then to Joseph's old room. It seemed lighter, empty. The rows of jars and plant stems were gone, as were the large sheets of paper and drawing supplies. Joseph's familiar smell barely lingered in the air.

Celeste quickly climbed the drapes. From this sill, a floor lower, she had a better view of the yard below.

Audubon and Joseph were checking and rechecking the ropes and leather straps. Then they turned to shake hands with Mr. Pirrie.

Celeste knew she could never get there in time. And even if she could, would Joseph see her in the grass? Wouldn't she just be flattened under the feet of the horses? Or chased across the grass by the cat? Or sniffed out by Dash and eaten in one gulp?

She could barely hear the voices of the men, but she knew they were saying words of parting. She saw Joseph lift his head toward his old bedroom window and imagined that his gaze lingered for a second. She raced back and forth along the windowsill. "Joseph! Joseph!" she squeaked.

But a moment more and both Joseph and Audubon were astride their horses, Dash tagging behind. Joseph kept looking back over his shoulder toward the house. Celeste watched them ride down the lane. She watched until the bend in the road hid them from view and they disappeared.

She made her way back up the attic steps. Home.

She positioned her chair on the sill, then sat watching as the sun touched the treetops.

She thought about Joseph: his skill at making a drawing, at making the painting of a leaf or flower look real, as though it were resting on the paper.

She thought about his kindness: The gentle way he

gave her a home in his pocket.

She pondered: Was it worth the feelings of sadness and melancholy to make a friend and then lose him? Would she rather not have the heartache of losing a friend and not have the memory of friendship? No, she decided, no.

She heard a fluttering sound from above her head.

She looked up to see a small bird peering down at her from the edge of the roof.

"Hello!" Celeste called up.

"Hello!" the bird chirped back. "Are you Celeste?"

Celeste smiled. "Yes, that's me! Who are you?"

With another fluttering of wings the little wren dropped to the sill. Her feathers were honey brown, and her eyes twinkled.

"My name is Violet," she said. "Pardon me for dropping in like this. I'm a friend of Cornelius."

"Cornelius! How wonderful! Welcome!" Celeste hurriedly scrambled to drag out another chair from the living room. "Is he all right? Have you heard from him?"

"Oh, he's quite a ways from here by now; I'm sure of that. We won't see him again until spring comes back. But he told me about you before he left. He said I'd find you here."

"I'm going to miss Cornelius this winter."

"He said you were the very best there is at finding dogwood berries," Violet said.

Celeste smiled. "Well, I don't know about that!"

"He told me you were a music lover."

"Cornelius is the one who made me realize how much I liked music."

"And he said you might like having a friend around this winter," said the wren.

"Well, he was right about that." Celeste chuckled.

She set out her blue-and-white china plates and filled them with tidbits from the cupboard.

"You have a beautiful nest," Violet said admiringly. "How did you come to live here?" And Celeste told her the story, all the way from the beginning.

The two sat gazing contentedly at the surrounding landscape. They heard the creaking wagons returning

from the fields, the jingle and clank of horse harnesses. Lafayette, silhouetted against the sky, flying with familiar flaps and glides, was returning from a fishing foray along the river; Celeste waved.

She smiled.

She thought about the summer, of surviving a terrible thunderstorm and of flying in a basket.

She thought of Mr. Audubon, and of secretly helping create a work of art.

She thought of Joseph, and how love can start with something as simple as the gift of a peanut.

She thought of Cornelius and Lafayette; and as she offered a berry to Violet, she thought how good it was to have friends.

Osprey and Weakfish (1829)

AFTERWORD

JOHN JAMES AUDUBON (1785–1851) was a master at creating powerful images filled with beauty and emotion, even though his subjects were merely birds. He spent most of his life traveling over much of eastern North America, often on foot, carrying paints and paper, sketching constantly, documenting the native plants and animals as they existed in the early 1800s.

Before Audubon came along, wildlife artists painted their subjects in static and stiff poses, as though mounted in a display case. But Audubon filled each of his paintings with a zest and vigor that makes them seem to fly across the page. This was years before photography, so his paintings are a record of animals and plants of another century. And his artistic ability was self-taught, which makes his work even more amazing.

The landscape that inspired him looked much different than it does today. Roads were scarce; this was long before the age of the automobile. Completion of the transcontinental railroad was still decades away. The population of the United

States was only around ten million; that's only about four people per square mile if you sprinkled them evenly over the country. Today, the population is more than thirty times that, a density of nearly eighty people per square mile.

Audubon walked or rode horseback through vast tracts of forest that stretched from the Atlantic Ocean to the Mississippi River, through deep woods of ancient, towering trees hundreds of years old. Thousands of miles of pristine rivers and millions of acres of woodland habitat had not yet been replaced or polluted by farms and industry. That would come later.

Along those rivers roamed animals we wouldn't expect to see there today: cougars and jaguars, wolves and bison, lynx and elk. Audubon encountered birds that are now extinct, such as the ivory-billed woodpecker, the Carolina parakeet, and the passenger pigeon mentioned in this story.

For nearly two years he traveled with an assistant, Joseph Mason. Joseph was a great help to Audubon; and although only a teenager (he was thirteen when he started out with Audubon), he became very skilled at painting botanical subjects, particularly wildflowers. Many of the beautiful backgrounds of plants and flowers in the bird portraits are credited to Joseph.

Audubon's life as a painter and naturalist was often difficult: He was separated from his family for long periods of time while out gathering specimens for his paintings, frequently living hand-to-mouth. No one was paying him to paint birds; it was his idea and his passion. But he managed to paint more than four hundred North American bird species, each one a carefully rendered portrait—from the dowdy field sparrow to the flamboyant flamingo.

It's a bit ironic that his paintings depict such lively, animated birds. His artistic methodology would be illegal today! He killed nearly all of his subjects, using a shotgun, and did indeed use wire to position the dead specimens into lifelike poses. His images were huge, all of them life-size; the pages of his *Birds of America* were nearly three feet tall, so large that two people were needed to turn the pages carefully, and special tables were required to display the books.

In 1821 Audubon lived for about four months at Oakley Plantation, not far from New Orleans, Louisiana. To earn his room and board while staying at Oakley he gave the plantation owner's daughter, Eliza Pirrie, dancing and drawing lessons. By reading his journals, we know that Audubon was particularly charmed and inspired by the woods and bayous around Oakley and worked diligently on many of his paintings at the plantation.

The fictionalized events in the story of Celeste take place during those four months. Some of it is true: Joseph was indeed shot while out flushing turkeys during a hunt, for example; and Audubon did keep a live ivory-billed woodpecker and a live osprey for a time.

But did Joseph have a field mouse for a companion? Was Eliza's old dollhouse tucked away in the attic? I like to think so.

I am so fortunate to have honest, encouraging, thoughtful, and talented friends who have spent many hours of their time reading drafts of this story and kindly giving me helpful suggestions. Many, many thanks to Quinn Keeler, Laura Behm, Nancy Powell, Roland Smith, Margaret Elliot, and Nan Fry.

Thank you, Amy Ryan, for your marvelous enthusiasm and energy with the design and layout.

And to my wonderful editor and friend, Katherine Tegen, with much love and appreciation, I dedicate this book.